ABSOLUTE ESSENCE

Christopher Guhl

PUBLISHER'S NOTE

This is a work of fiction. All names, places, characters, and incidences are either the product of the author's imagination, or are used fictitiously, and any resemblance to actual people, alive or dead, events or locations, is completely coincidental.

A product of PAPER STAR PUBLISHING LLC

ISBN (Paperback): 978-1-7345782-0-1

ISBN (eBook): 978-1-7345782-1-8

ChristopherGuhl.com

Cover art by ARTAUXEO
Cover lettering by Christian Bentulan
Illustrations by Antonio Baldari

Dedicated to my best friends. You all know who you are.

Absolute Essence | Christopher Guhl

Chapter One

Tem tried rubbing a dirt stain from his shirt while he waited at the edge of the market. *Ugh, this is my favorite shirt too!* He looked up and caught Neema squeezing her way through the crowd toward the power stonc booth. Kids didn't have money to spend, so no one in the market paid either of them any mind. She looked back and scratched her eye, then pulled her ear.

Looks like the plan is a go!

He sidestepped an old lady trying to sneak ahead in the baca fruit line, then cracked his knuckles while waiting for Neema's next signal. A man from the back of the line began hollering, giving Tem the chance to slide through and keep an eye on Neema.

She flipped her hair back over her shoulder, splashing teal highlights against her back.

The signal!

Tem stole another look at Neema's hair, he'd been doing that more lately, then darted toward the booth. People cursed and yelled at him, one young woman spilling her entire bag of melons. They thudded to the ground and rolled every which way.

Tem whizzed past Neema to the stall and grabbed a handful of power chips out of the merchant's display, then tipped the whole box over, spilling power chips in front of the booth. Tem laughed and took off through the market again.

"Hey!" the merchant yelled. "Get back here, you little prick!"

Tem looked back and snickered.

The merchant called for his guard, then looked down and cursed at the power chips scattered on the ground. The big, burly thug barreled through the crowd with no regard for who he trampled in his pursuit.

It was a good thing Tem was fast, because he couldn't knock people down even if he tried. Tem was thin as a rail, so he maneuvered between everyone, making his way through the market.

"Where's an alley!?" Tem asked himself, searching through the thinning crowd for a way to escape the gaining thug. He looked over to an opening down to the sewers.

Not that again, he thought. *Neema said I stunk like shit for a week!*

"There's gotta be a better way!"

Just as he had a good idea, his hopes deflated.

"Hey, you! Halt!" Three city watchmen saw Tem kicking up dust and ran after him, parting the crowd ahead of them.

"Kst!" Tem spat, turning down a side street.

He spared a glance behind him. *At least the thug is gone.*

The bad news was watchmen were harder to get rid of, especially if they called in a mindless soldier. Tem had to ditch them, fast.

Flickering, yellow neon caught Tem's eye like it was waving at him. *Yes!* He knew this place. It was an old bar with an alley around back that had piping leading all the way to the roof. He cut into the alley and jumped for the piping, kicking against one wall. The pipes groaned from his weight, but didn't budge. He lifted himself up the wall, climbing it like it were the side of a mountain. Voices rose from the alley below, but Tem was already lifting himself over the edge of the building.

Whew!

The rooftops were level enough, so Tem jumped across each one. It was as good as flying, and in a matter of seconds he was over a block away from the watchmen. Up there, he could see the whole city, even the golden palace towers in the distance. Everything aside from the palace was a dreadful gray or black, matching the clouds overhead that never seemed to go away. Soon he was back to an alley by the front gate of the market, sliding down a set of pipes to the mud. He slipped and rolled, then noticed a shadow rise above him. Tem looked up just in time to see a fist slam into his face.

The punch sent Tem tumbling across the ground, splattering mud on the already crusted walls. "You think yuh so clevuh," a deep voice with a heavy accent said. Tem's vision dazed and filled with spots, but it was clear enough that he could make out his attacker. It was the thug from the power stone booth. "Runnin so fast, jumpin across rooftops. Now I got yuh."

Tem didn't waste time. "You want em? You can have em!" He reached in his pocket and hurled the power chips at the thug. Some of them bounced off his heavy chest, but others flew out into the market.

The thug fumbled at the power chips and tried to grab Tem as he ran by, but came up with nothing but mud.

Comin through! Tem said to himself as he disappeared back into the crowd.

*****

Neema didn't even watch as Tem sped away.

He knows what he's doing, she told herself, staying close to the power stone stall. The owner muttered curses as he brushed the fallen power chips into a pile to scoop up. No one noticed as she walked behind him to a power chip that fell close to the edge of the stall.

She reached down and picked it up, flipping it between her fingers. It gleamed red in what light dared show itself between all the clouds overhead in Essence City.

"Excuse me, sir?" Neema knelt next to where the man was on his knees brushing chips back into his display box.

"What!?" he cursed, then looked up and saw Neema with her sweet smile.

"I found this over there." She handed him the power chip and batted her eyelashes like a butterfly's wings.

The man's mouth stuck open for a second, long enough that Neema smelled his nasty breath. He chuckled to himself. "If only all the young kids were as honest as you, sweetheart."

She smiled back, flipped the chip in his box, and turned around to head back. Once she was out of the market, she pulled two large power stones out of her handbag, letting them shine in the streetlight. These stones could power an entire household for over a month. She stuck out her tongue. *Too easy.*

*****

Tem cursed himself for ruining his shirt while he walked the damp streets to their hiding spot. *I wonder if Neema's mom could wash it out?* he thought.

"Took you long enough," Neema said after he trudged up the fire escape and dragged himself through the window. She sat on a windowsill nearby, fiddling with the wiring on a control pad. It was an empty office space they found in an abandoned warehouse near the harbor.

"Three watchmen got in my way, and then that stupid guard came back and decked me." Tem cursed himself for letting the guard get the jump on him and rubbed his swollen eye.

Neema gasped when she looked up and saw Tem's face. Jumping down from the windowsill, she reached up and gently traced the blackening around his eye. Tem tried not to look at her, but her face was so close to his. His eyes drifted to the way a strand of her hair curled down to her cheek. Neema licked her thumb and wiped a spot under his eye.

Tem turned away, making Neema laugh. Her violet eyes brightened, and Tem had to resist from staring.

"So what'd you get?" Tem asked.

Neema pulled two power stones from her bag, and Tem's eyes widened. He didn't even care that he lost out on the chips.

"The poor old fool set em down right as you ran by," Neema said. "Didn't even notice."

Tem smiled, "Do you think…"

"Phase three?"

"Totally! Let's go check!"

They got up and ran out of the room to a hallway that was little more than scaffolding. Tem grabbed the railing and looked down on the open warehouse.

"You ever wonder how lucky we are to have this all to ourselves?" he asked.

Neema scoffed. "Lucky that the warehouse has been shut down and abandoned because the king wants more workers for the stone refineries? Hardly, but yeah, it works out for us, huh?"

Tem reddened and thought about the rest of the desolate buildings by the harbor. *Yeah, the king is a jerk.*

"How's that control pad comin?" Tem asked as they walked toward the stairs. "Weren't you gonna work on the interior today too?"

"Yeah, but I kept hearin stuff, so I didn't wanna go inside until you got here."

Tem nodded. They had to be careful about keeping their project a secret and under wraps, stacking all the remaining garbage and empty barrels around it and covering it with a tarp to keep it hidden. Even looking at it from above, it blended in with the rest of the debris.

The steps rattled as Tem stomped his way to the ground floor where a wall of barrels and conglomeration of tarps kept their project hidden like a makeshift fort. It gave them room to work, build, and test. Tem stepped underneath a dangling river of wires to walk inside the workspace.

"Awesome…" Tem whispered, looking up at their project. "Who'da thought we could build our own *airship*!" The makeshift lights above cast a golden outline around the ship.

"That's because *I* did most of the work," Neema said, smiling back at him.

"Hey! I helped!"

Neema started connecting the control panel to the dashboard and laughed. "You did such a good job stealing your dad's blueprints so I could figure out how to make all this stuff!"

Tem could barely remember when his father was an engineer before the last yurdrak attack. He used most of those old blueprints as drawing paper before finding this one thrown in the garbage.

Tem grabbed his hammer and started smoothing out a piece of metal he wanted to use on the remaining wing. "And?"

"I suppose those arms of yours helped a little, banging away with that hammer of yours."

"That's right!" he said, "and now we're almost done."

"'Almost' if you mean we're missing a wing, the wiring is a disaster, and we still haven't even flown the damn thing!" Neema laughed. "But yeah, it's lookin better." She put her hands on her hips and admired the hunk of machinery for a moment, nodding.

Tem shifted his eyes from her to the sheet of metal and back. Just then she shook out her hair and ran her hand through it, arching her back.

Crunch! He slammed the hammer down on his thumb. "Achhh!" he cried out. It was already red and throbbing, soon it would swell twice its size.

Neema ran over, a confused look spreading across her face. "What the hell, Tem? How do you smash your finger!?"

He already felt his ears burning, so he turned away from her and shook out his hand. "I'm fine!"

They continued working in silence for a little while. Tem finished smoothing out the metal pieces for the wing, and he started attaching the brackets for the seats.

"Think we can fit everyone in?" Neema asked. She was still working on the wiring harness, adding in the stolen power stones. They planned on bringing Neema's parents and Tem's father with them.

"Yeah, I'll make sure we get em all in," he replied. "Gonna rig up a special chair for pa." He looked at one bracket and thought out loud for a moment. "Hmm, suppose we could make it so he can lock in his wheelchair."

"Well," Neema started, standing up and stretching. "The wiring harness should be done. Too bad it doesn't fix how ugly this thing is!"

Tem scoffed. She was always teasing about how ugly the airship was. He stepped down from the ship and looked back at it, smiling. Then he shrugged.

Yeah, it is *ugly.*

But then again, the airship was basically made of garbage. He smirked, looking up at the trash can he repurposed as an exhaust vent.

"Just needs a little paint," Tem said, wrapping his arms behind his head. "Think it'll work?" He stepped toward where Neema was curling up some wires, and she cautioned him to stay back.

"Woah, woah there, hotshot. Remember the last time you tried to help me with this? It took the rest of the night to get you untangled!"

Tem nodded and stepped back. That night he somehow had wires in places where wires shouldn't be.

"Okay, ya just gonna stand there with that dumb look on your face, or are ya gonna get back to work?"

"What? Oh, right." Tem was still thinking about wires, so he grabbed his hammer and sauntered off.

"Now, I've got to rerun a few things, but give me an hour and I think we can turn it on."

"Ah! It's gonna be bad ass!" Tem said. He had everything planned out. "Once it's all done-"

"The wing?" Neema interrupted, pointing at the stack of junk metal.

"Yeah, yeah!" Tem said, grabbing a piece and hammering away. "We'll fly out at night. No other airships should be around. Just gonna head out over the harbor, then swing around and fly north." Tem daydreamed the image, basking in the sun, his arm around Neema, and the entire world his for the taking. "Then we learn how to *really* live!"

"Pff! You wouldn't know how. But… once we finish that wing, get a propeller, then steal a few more power stones, I think we should be good. A wind stone would be helpful, but we'd probably get killed trying to steal one. Aghh!" Sparks flew from where Neema was working underneath the dash of the ship's cabin, skittering across the floor before disappearing. "Stupid thing!"

"You all right!?" Tem asked.

She waved her hand at him, then got back underneath the dash. "Oh, hey! When do we have to meet up with your dad for studies?"

"I think you mean teach ourselves while he drinks old man Sosa's moonshine," Tem said. "We've got a few hours. He's probably still sleeping."

Neema didn't have to say it. It was different when Tem's mother was still alive and taught them.

They continued working for about half an hour when Tem heard the bells, but Neema was waist deep in the airship's fuselage, humming to herself.

"Neema!" She looked up, her violet eyes gleaming in the dim light.

He nodded up, motioning to listen. Her eyes opened wider, and she dropped a tangle of wires.

"A yurdrak!?" She gathered her things, just as Tem did. "Is it just a drill? I don't remember one scheduled for today."

"There wasn't." Tem knew. He knew when *all* the yurdrak drills were. It had been two years since the last onslaught, and seven since he was left motherless and his father in a wheelchair.

Father! Tem worried. The man never cared whether he'd live through any future attack, but Tem needed to keep him alive, if only to save the only family he had.

"But they only attack every five years, why so soon?"

Tem couldn't think about that or anything else. All he let himself think of was making sure the people he cared about would be okay. As they sprinted out of the abandoned warehouse, a squad of waterminds rushed by. Some of them surfed against the buildings or on the ground. Water splashed at Tem and Neema, soaking their clothes. If waterminds were this close to them that meant the yurdrak wouldn't be far.

"Waterminds…" Neema said. "It's a firedrak! Not good."

Fire was one of the most devastating elements when controlled by a beast like a yurdrak. They were terrible creatures, leaving only misery, destruction, and death in their tracks.

Tem froze at the memory of the last and only time he ever saw a yurdrak, when a waterdrak flooded half the city with a massive wave blast. Tem's father brought him to a nearby shelter, but his mom was working late at the factory.

She was on her way home when the blast hit, he recalled. *They found her body a week later.*

"Tem!" Neema called. She outpaced him as they ran through the streets to their apartment complex.

"Yeah!" He pushed harder to catch up.

Maybe this one won't be too bad, he hoped. *The last one didn't even make it inside the city. What element was it again? Wind…*

Tem could see their apartment complex at the end of the long street. It didn't have its own shelter. That was another block down.

Gotta make sure Pa made it out, Tem told himself.

Before he finished his thought, a grumbling noise overpowered all the

14

other commotion. It rose to a full on roar, loud enough to make the ground tremble. Tem's heart jumped and his mouth went dry. He didn't want to look, but he had to. It was too tempting. With one quick glance, he saw the beast rise from the other side of a building a block behind them.

The airship! There was nothing Tem could do but hope the beast wouldn't destroy it. Smoke rose from its skin. It's whole body looked like a carved piece of dark charcoal, with flaming eyes and fire that spewed from its mouth.

"Don't look!" Neema yelled back.

"Hmph!" Tem nodded, turning back to catch up. They weren't far from the shelter. If only they could-

A watermind flew in front of them and rolled across the pavement, trails of smoke coming off his charred body.

Tem stopped, looming over the watermind's body.

"What are you doing?" Neema asked, waving her arms. "We've gotta go!"

"He's alive! We can help him!"

The watermind was just a young man, maybe a few years older than Tem. His eyes were sea blue and cloudy, with no pupils. Tem had never seen a mindless soldier up close. Tem didn't know what to do outside of watch the watermind's labored breaths.

"Come on, Tem! Let's go!" Neema was pulling his arm now.

The yurdrak roared again, and Tem stumbled as the ground shook beneath him. He heard the splash and sizzle of water on fire as the waterminds continued their assault on the creature. Neema pulled Tem back up just as the injured watermind rolled to his side, revealing more burns, slashes, and purple bruises.

"There's no way he can keep fighting," Tem said. "Not looking like that!"

The watermind stood and tensed his muscles, looking over Tem's shoulder toward the yurdrak. He wore only a pair of thin pants, no boots or shirt, Tem knew people living on the street with more to protect them. The watermind took a deep breath and turned.

"No!" Tem cried. "You can't go! You're hurt! Come with us." Tem grabbed the man's arm, but the watermind pulled away with no regard for Tem or Neema's presence. With a surging wave, the watermind took off.

Tem didn't realize it, but he turned toward the fighting like he would join the watermind. Neema shouted at him and tugged at his arm, urging him to give it up and run away.

Why would that watermind go back? Tem thought. The only thing back there was death. *Maybe when boys turn into mindless soldiers they do lose their minds. I'll be long gone from this place before that happens to me.*

Neema gave Tem another pull, and they ran off away from the yurdrak and the flame blasts it hurled in every direction.

"We've gotta get to that shelter!" Neema yelled. "That thing could be right back on top of us like that!" She snapped her fingers as she ran.

Just as she did, Tem heard a crack echo through the streets, but didn't dare turn to see the terror behind him. He didn't have to. The building that they were running by started to fall, raining stone debris in a deafening downpour.

Neema screamed, she was closest to the building, so Tem grabbed her and rolled. Flames surrounded and licked at them, kissing their skin. The building crushed down in pieces the size of Tem's apartment, creating a maze of fiery debris.

It's so hot! he thought, remembering a night he got too close to a burning candle. He believed then that was the hottest thing he'd ever feel. He was wrong. Pieces of the building behind them began to disintegrate, leaving behind nothing but ash and spreading fire.

"There!" Neema shouted, pointing at a cave-like opening in the debris. Tem held her hand, guiding her toward it through the burning flames. The building behind him was disintegrating from the heat, so they crawled and inched their way away from it. As they emerged on the other side they met the same scene. Fire burned all around them, and they both choked and gagged in the smoke. Even the ground beneath Tem's feet was hot enough to keep him from staying in one place for too long.

Then a massive wave doused the whole block, putting out the fires with a sizzle.

"What is that!?" Neema yelled.

"I don't know, I can't see!" Tem cried. Fog covered the entire block.

The steam cooled, and a gentle mist trickled in, soothing Tem's skin. As he looked over his wounds, he noticed someone watching him from the corner of his eye.

"Hey!" Tem called out, recognizing the watermind from before. He rode a wave that rose with the steam. Before Tem could call out again, the young man vanished.

Maybe he's not so mindless.

"Did you see that!?" Tem asked.

"I can't see anything!" Neema replied. She was down on one knee, shielding her face.

"Are you okay?"

She peered from underneath her raised arm, and there was something different about the way she looked up at him. Was it fear? Relief? Or something else?

It made Tem's stomach feel funny. He reached down and helped her to her feet, her touch making his blood rush. She brushed off some soot that collected all over her body. Looking down at himself he realized he was caked in it too. He brushed it off as best he could, but with all the moisture around it just stuck to his hands.

"Aghh!" he growled, to which Neema responded with laughter.

"Wha-" he began to say, but just then she rubbed her finger on his nose, coating it in soot.

"Hey!"

"Come on," she nodded toward the end of the block. "Looks like the yurdrak's moving on. We should get out of here while we can."

"You think it's still standing?" Tem asked as they ran down the street, curving in and around chunks of surrounding buildings.

"I don't know," was all Neema replied with.

As they closed in on the end of the street, Tem got the sinking feeling that the apartment was gone. Rubble coated the street, and most of the buildings were in ruin. They climbed up over another jutting slab of concrete and turned the corner. Tem fell to his knees. The building was still there.

"See?" Neema said, urging him back up again. "Everything's okay! Come on!" Neema had a brighter outlook on everything.

How does she do that?

"Looks empty!" Neema called back, but he ran down the hall anyway, leaving her in the doorway. He had to *see*.

The door to their apartment was open, but it was as Neema predicted. Empty.

"Please be okay, Pa." Tem said. "Alright, let's get to the shelter!"

Just as Tem finished his sentence, the windows erupted with light, blinding him.

"Ahhh!" he cried, but the pained screaming of the monster overpowered any noise. The building shook, bits of the ceiling fell, and Tem dropped to the floor. The very air inside the apartment burned as hot as the beast itself. Tem knew that the yurdrak was right outside.

"Neema!" he called out. *Where is she!?*

Tem looked down the hall, and saw that the doorway to the apartment caved in. *Neema was just there!* He tromped through the hall, tripping and bouncing off the walls the whole way.

"Neema!" There she was outside the apartment, sprawled on the ground, unmoving.

He ran to her side, hovering over her. "Come on, wake up!" Her chest rose and fell, but she wouldn't respond, even when he shook her. "We gotta go, Neema! We gotta go!" Judging by the sweat pouring down his face, the yurdrak had to be right on top of them.

"I'm gonna get you outta here, Neema." He scooped her up in his arms and stood. *She looks so small,* he thought, looking down at her curled up against him. He started for the shelter, stomping down the street one step at a time. "Don't worry," he told her. "There'll be a doctor at the shelter, and they're gonna get ya all patched up!"

The hot air all around him blasted him like he was in the middle of a furnace. Inch by inch, he trudged through the sweltering heat as the ground shook, buildings fell, and the battle between monster and man raged.

Don't think about that, he commanded himself. *Just go!* He spit through clenched teeth, eyes straining to stay open as he neared the end of the block.

"Rahhhh! We're gonna make it, Neema!" he yelled. "I'm gonna get you there!"

The yurdrak roared, and his whole body trembled from the noise. It was like it was right on top of him! He nearly dropped Neema, but he kept his arms clamped around her.

"I won't let go!" he said. "I'll never let go."

Then he saw it. The yurdrak's gigantic paw crashed down, smashing the corner of a building across the street from the shelter entrance. Fire bounced and skittered, setting the building aflame. Tem trembled with each step and his tears felt like hot grease rolling down his cheek. Mindless soldiers flooded the street, swarming around the monster like flies at the fruit stands in the market.

Keep going!

He barged through the entrance and descended the stairs, somehow keeping his footing. With one last look before the door closed behind him, the yurdrak turned away and moved as quick as a dancing flame to the other side of the neighborhood. No yurdrak had lasted this long against the mindless. This had to be one of the most powerful to attack the city.

Tem was so dazed he didn't realize he was banging on the shelter doors. They finally opened, and he rushed in, passing everyone. People tried to talk to him, but he didn't listen. Someone tried to take Neema from him, but he wouldn't, he couldn't, let her go.

"It's okay, boy," someone said. "I can help her."

"Okay!" he said. "Help her. F-father? Where..."

"Neema!" a voice called. Tem recognized the man. Neema's father. "Is she okay?"

"Looks like it's just a hit on the head," the doctor said. "Maybe a few burns too. She'll be fine, but she'll have a massive headache."

"Tem," her father said as he focused on Neema while she rested.

"Tem!" Tem snapped out of his daze and looked up. "Your father is here, son. Down the hall."

Tem nodded and stood. Stars popped in front of his eyes, and his vision turned purple and red. After one step he fell to the ground on one knee. The voices around him sounded like they were underwater. He pushed off his knee to get up and start walking again, but this time he fell straight to the ground. The purples and reds darkened until he couldn't see anymore.

Chapter Two

Neema sat with her father and scratched at the bandage on the side of her head. It throbbed like the yurdrak was squishing it between its claws like a grape. She'd been unconscious for a couple hours. The last thing she remembered was telling Tem everything would be okay. How wrong she was.

She cringed looking at the burns that covered Tem's body as one of the older women worked on him. Somehow, he carried Neema from the apartment to the shelter while the yurdrak was battling with the mindless army. The older folk were saying it was a miracle he made it.

"Don't worry about him, dear," her father said, returning with a fresh cup of coffee. "He's in good hands."

"Is the yurdrak still out there?"

He shook his head. "They're saying it fled the city. We'll stay here until we get the all clear. The mindless will take care of the yurdrak, whether they do it here or in the country."

Neema looked back to Tem. She'd owe him one now, and that made her smile. Usually she was the one getting *him* out of tight spots. *Great,* she thought, *he'll never let me live this down.* She walked up and stood closer to his bed. The woman putting salve and bandages on him didn't pay Neema any mind.

So peaceful. It was an odd look for him.

"He'll be just fine, dear," the woman said.

Neema didn't take her eyes off him. "I know."

"A special boy, this one. You're lucky."

"Why's that?"

"I don't think he would've carried just anyone that far in those conditions. A right lad, this one. Hang on to im."

Neema ignored the lady and walked up to Tem's father, who was watching from the corner of the room. He eyed her as she approached. Tem's father always made her uncomfortable, even when Tem was around.

"I don't wanna hear it, girl," he said. "I almost lost my boy because ah you. I already lost my wife and my legs. Those damn creatures. They'll never stop."

"Sir-"

"Leave me be, girl." He leveled his eyes at her. She couldn't respond. The man never liked her. He didn't like anything. Except for whatever drink old man Sosa cooked up. Even then, in front of everyone, he was taking swigs from his flask. Neema couldn't understand the urge, maybe she never would. It was all the man held on to. Tem worked so hard to make sure that the two of them would be okay, but every night the man threw it away in drink.

Neema narrowed her eyes at him, but he didn't see her. He was here in the room, but his mind was somewhere else. It wasn't right that Tem was suffering now, and his father wasted himself away in drink. Neema wanted to kick his wheelchair, but she resisted the urge.

"Stupid man," she muttered, walking away to wait with her parents.

The all clear sounded about an hour later, so everyone left aside from her and the nurses, waiting for Tem to wake up. Neema thought about the upcoming draft. They will recruit more boys to replace the mindless soldiers lost in battle. Boys forced to leave their families and friends. The families get some compensation, but at what cost? *They never return...*

"That won't happen to us," she told Tem as he slept. Girls weren't chosen, and Tem was too young. "It works out better this way. There won't be another attack for a few years, and by then we'll be outta here!"

Other people stopped by the shelter throughout the day, bringing well wishes and gossip. One woman, a younger gal that spoke fast and revealed a blushing amount of cleavage, spoke of a rebellion to the north.

"Yeah! They're hiding out in the jungles way past the king's reach. I wonder what it's like up there."

"A yurdrak attack *and* a rebellion?" the nurse exclaimed as she changed Tem's bandages. "That's too much!"

"Umm hum," the gossip replied, adjusting her shirt, "and tomorrow the king is making an announcement."

"That must mean the army killed that yurdrak. About time." She finished with Tem's bandages and stood, unbuttoning her nurse's robe and tossing it aside. "Well, honey. Morla's shift starts in a few, but I'm gonna take off early. You good here on your own, right?"

She didn't wait for an answer as her and the cleavage-laden gossip stalked out of the room, moving on to do whatever women their age did when night approached.

Neema scooted closer to Tem, examining his features. His messy, blonde hair covered his eyes, so she moved some strands out of the way. Her hand paused at his cheek, and she glided her thumb over his lips.

"You've changed the past few months," she whispered. "Sometimes you're so distant, but then other times you're risking your life for mine."

She thought about kissing him. *Maybe it'll wake you up like it does in those silly fairytales.*

She inched closer to his face, wondering what a kiss would feel like. "What am I to you?" she asked. No one was around, and Tem would never know. She reached out with her lips, trying to grasp his. Just a little bit further...

Tem's chest heaved, and he drew in a deep breath. His eyes shot open. Neema gasped and backed away, retracting her hand to her chest.

"Wha-" Tem had trouble getting the words out. His voice was hoarse and raspy. "What h-happened?"

*****

Tem felt like he'd been drug through the street with no clothes, then thrown in the oven to cook with dinner. Neema hovered awfully close to him. "Something on my face?"

Neema's face paled and her eyes shot to the floor as she lowered herself back into her chair. "I'm sorry to have to tell you this, but-"

"What is it? My father! Is he?" Devastating thoughts raced through Tem's mind.

Neema raised a hand to quiet him. "He's okay. It's your face. During the yurdrak attack-"

Tem tried reaching for his face, but it hurt to move his arms. He couldn't even sit up straight without his muscles screaming in pain. Neema held up a mirror to show him.

"You're so ugly you scared the yurdrak away!" Neema cackled.

He tried to find something to throw at her, but there was nothing within reach. Instead, he shot her a nasty look and folded his arms in front of his chest, turning away.

"Oh, come on!" she pushed on his back. "You walked into that one!"

Tem leaned back over and noticed the bandage on her forehead. He nodded up to it, "What about you?"

She reached up and patted the bandage, then shrugged her shoulders. "No biggie."

Tem nodded and started to sit up. "Same here, so whattaya say? Wanna go snag some loot? Best time is after a yurdrak attack."

Neema tilted her head, frowning. "You're supposed to stay in bed, young man."

"And who are you, my doctor?" He stood up, wavering for a moment before he started for the other side of the room. Neema's giggles behind him caused him to stop and turn. "What is it now?"

She stifled her giggling and turned away, pressing her lips together. "Nothing. I like your gown is all. It's cute."

"What are you-" he stopped talking when he looked down at himself. All he wore was a thin gown with nothing underneath. It opened up on the backside, giving Neema a front row view of his butt.

His face turned as hot as the damned yurdrak, and Neema burst out laughing. There wasn't enough material to cover himself, so he looked around for his clothes.

The door to his room burst open, and Tem about fell as the nurse barged in.

"What's going on in here!?" she asked. "You're not supposed to be out of bed!"

Tem stammered, but couldn't get any words out. The nurse grabbed his ear and led him back into bed, muttering to herself the whole way.

"And what are you still doing here?" the nurse asked Neema, cutting her laughter short.

"Sorry, ma'am," Neema replied. "The other nurse said I could stay."

The nurse put a hand on her hip. "She still here?"

"Um, no. She left early."

"Exactly. Now scram! It's too late for a young girl like you to be out in this city."

"Yes, ma'am." She smiled once more at Tem before rushing out the door. "Now you stay here and don't move. I'll be back in a little while to replace those bandages."

The nurse made good on her promise, as she returned three times throughout the night to change out Tem's bandages. It wasn't until late the next morning, after Tem promised her five times that he'd change them himself, that she let him put some clothes on and go home.

"And tell your daddy I'll come over there if I have to!" she called out to him as he ascended the shelter steps.

Neema leaned against the wall of the shelter outside, looking up at the sky.

"Took you long enough," she said.

"Mhmm." Tem joined her against the wall and raised his eyes to the sky. There was nothing but gray clouds, like always. They swirled and stormed and rained, but never left. Neema's mother told them there was a beautiful, blue sky beyond the clouds. Sometimes Tem could see the outline of the sun on boiling days after a heavy storm, but couldn't picture what it might look like without the cloud cover.

Neema kicked herself off the wall and shoved her hands in her pockets. "Ready?"

Truth was, Tem was still reeling from getting his clothes on, but he

27

nodded anyway. They walked along the streets back toward where the yurdrak wreaked havoc, passing charred ruins of what used to be their neighborhood.

"How about that?" Neema pointed to a pile of junk on the street corner.

Tem frowned. It all looked terribly heavy, and he was sore from keeping pace with Neema. "Nah," he said, "let's keep looking."

Neema shrugged, "You're right. Gotta keep on the lookout for the good stuff!" She rubbed her hands together, her eyes glimmering as they searched for better loot.

"There's probably nothin left now," he said, cursing himself for getting hurt. *Should've stayed in bed at this rate.*

"Hey now! You never know. We might stumble onto a stash of wind stones. Then we'd be hitting phase four like that!" She snapped her fingers.

"Yeah!" Tem agreed. "Wait… what's phase four again?"

She pushed him, nearly knocking him over, but he played it off like it was nothing. "Testing, silly! After that, we're home free."

They walked further, picking up good pieces of scrap metal along the way until Tem's scrap sack overflowed, forcing him to walk with a limp. One of the sandwich shops Tem liked to eat at was nothing more than blackened rubble, and most of the lower neighborhoods were flooded. Few were untouched, but still a jumbled mess of buildings, houses, and complexes so close they might as well have been stacked on top of each other.

"The old people talk about a rebellion up north," Neema told him. "Could you imagine?"

"No way!" Tem exclaimed. "I wonder how they made it out of the city. Not everyone can build an airship like us!"

"And the only other people allowed outside the city are the mindless soldiers and the farmers, but even they're under constant watch."

"We'll just have to meet up with em and find out!"

"Hmph!" Neema nodded.

They continued, and as the day wore on Tem started dragging his scrap sack. Sweat built up as if his muscles were crying from the exhaustion, and all of his burns and bruises ached more and more with each step.

"You okay?" Neema asked.

"Yeah," Tem said, straightening himself. "We've already missed out on all the good stuff, gotta get what's left."

"The nurse said you shouldn't even be out of bed."

"Yeah, well the nurse can shove off!"

Neema giggled at that.

"You never know when there'll be another attack. One more minute in that damn bed is another minute I could live! Can't waste it, and once we're free it'll all be worth it."

Neema shrugged and nodded down a side street. "Well, the warehouse is just down that other street. Might as well drop off what we have at the airship, then keep going."

Tem couldn't argue with that, especially since a few metal beams he grabbed for the propeller kept whacking him in the face every other step. They stashed the hefty bag of material inside the warehouse and made sure the airship was still in one piece, aside from all the other pieces strewn about the warehouse they were working on.

"Hey," Neema said as they left. "How about a snack? My treat!"

"Hm?"

"Come on. I know a cool place not far from here. Just over by the docks."

He followed along, passing all the abandoned buildings. Most of the docks were empty, except for one that was bustling with people.

"People still go out on the water?" Tem asked.

"Yeah," Neema replied. "Not many, but they still find water stones out there when they're fishing, so the king allows it."

"Huh."

Neema took him to a small stand crowded with older, tattooed men.

Seamen, Tem thought, wondering what it was like to float around on a boat all day long.

When they got to the front of the line, an older woman looked down her crooked nose at them with a frown.

"Two frozen suisu fruits, please!" Neema smiled, melting the scowling old woman to butter.

"Sure thing, hun. Two chips."

Tem pulled out what money he had, but Neema held his arm down as she paid the woman.

"What gives!?" he asked.

"It's the least I can do," Neema said. "You know, for saving me and all." She wagged her shoulder, nudging him before grabbing the two treats.

They walked over to the dock, sat down, and dangled their legs over the deep, blue waters, licking their frozen snacks. There they sat watching and eating, not speaking amidst the surrounding sounds of dockworkers, waves, and wind. As Tem sucked on the last bit of his suisu fruit, he looked over at Neema, and the teal highlights in her hair lit up in the streetlights.

Now this is the life, Tem thought. For a moment, the pain from the multiple burns, cuts, and bruises didn't bother him.

"Hey, you kids!" the woman from the treat stand called out. "Better start on back home. The king's announcement and all."

Neema slurped off the last bit of her suisu fruit, and the two rushed toward home. Attendance from everyone was required.

"I wonder if the king actually speaks somewhere," Tem said, "or if he just sits on his fancy throne in the palace and lets his goons do it for him."

"Well he's never shown up in *our* neighborhood," Neema said. "I'll bet he sits there and stuffs his face with piles of food."

Tem grinned. "That's probably all he ever does. I'll bet he's *super* fat!"

The clouds up above were an alarming shade of gray, blanketing Essence City in darkness as the evening began. They neared their neighborhood's meeting location, an empty parking lot lit up with a few streetlights. All the surrounding streets and alleyways were dark.

"It's pretty busy," Neema said. "Oh, our parents!" She pointed them out in the crowd. It was easy to spot Tem's father against a fence in his wheelchair. Neema's parents stood at his side.

"Hello, father," Tem said, approaching at a slow gait.

"Mm," his father responded, nodding.

"Whattaya think this is all about?" Neema asked her dad.

He shrugged. "Not sure, hun. Hoping it's just news that they killed the yurdrak."

Her mother nodded, rubbing her hand on her dad's shoulder. They all waited in silence as curators took the census. Tem looked around at the faces of all the other families waiting and saw the same look he was sure was scrawled on his face. Anxiety, apprehension, and, worst of all, fear.

All eyes moved to the makeshift platform as the king's representative, a portly man with thick-rimmed glasses, walked up to deliver the news.

"Attention! Listen up! Your king is speaking through me." He unwound a scroll and began reading. "Citizens of Essence City. As your king, I hereby decree...

"Yesterday, a fire yurdrak, commonly known as a firedrak, attacked the city. It left many casualties in its wake, and parts of the city in ruin. The beast escaped capture and execution regardless of the numerous attempts by the King's Army. I have dispatched more soldiers to track the creature.

"The monster escaped because the quality of the mindless draftees has fallen to an unacceptable level. I will not tolerate this. Recruitment of new soldiers for the King's Army is required."

A few murmurs lifted in the air, and Tem noticed multiple guards posted at each corner of the lot.

They're recruiting? *Now!?* Tem thought, raising an eyebrow at Neema. She kept looking straight ahead at the man reading the scroll.

Usually recruitment came many months after the most recent yurdrak had fallen. *This attack must've been bad...*

He looked around at the other boys a couple years older than him. Some of them broke down and began to cry, some muttered curses. Others, the fools, grinned, holding their heads high like it was some honor to lose their minds. Sure, they'd gain incredible power, but Tem had never heard of a mindless soldier returning home from their years of service. The mothers of the boys old enough began embracing them, and it made Tem think of his own mother.

At least they're able to hug them and tell them goodbye, he told himself, thinking back to when she was killed. *I'll be long gone by the time it's my turn to be drafted.*

The man speaking called for silence and continued. "Furthermore. The strength of this firedrak calls for more intensive training for the newest recruits in the King's Army. I now order the minimum age for eligibility be lowered from the age of fifteen years to thirteen."

Tem's heart nearly stopped, the blood in his veins going cold. His world went silent. He looked over at Neema, and she was staring at him in shock. He turned to his father, and the man wouldn't even look up.

"No..." he whispered. *It's not supposed to be like this!*

The representative began reading names, and a chorus of crying mothers sang their sad songs. Fathers looked on weakly. Some shouted arguments, but those were dowsed as mindless soldiers appeared at the gates. There was no argument against the king's word. It was backed up by his army.

Neema's hand wrapped around his, and they stood together as the inevitable approached. Tem took it all in, committing everything about her to memory, the smoothness of her skin, the creases in her palm, the warmth of her touch.

Hearing his name called cut him as deep as when he found out his mother died, and it was as if that same old wound reopened.

He turned, wishing he could freeze that moment in time, so he could spend eternity looking into Neema's eyes. Tears crawled down her face. Her father and mother appeared on either side of her, their faces cast downward.

"Father..." Tem said.

His father held up a hand and turned away, shaking his head. Neema's dad pushed his glasses higher on the bridge of his nose, then stepped forward and placed a firm hand on Tem's shoulder. "Be careful out there, boy. We'll help look after your pa." He then shuffled Neema's mom and Tem's father away.

Guards appeared behind him, their very presence weighing on him. Neema grabbed his face with both hands, and she looked deep into his eyes like she was trying to burn an image of herself in them. Her violet eyes glistened with tears, and her face was pale.

She's so pretty, he thought.

"You can't give up," he said. "Finish the ship and get outta here."

Neema nodded. "I'll find you and free you. We'll go together!"

Always thinking positive. Tem forced a smile.

"Come on, boy," one guard behind him said. "Time to go."

"Goodbye, Neema," Tem said. She shook her head, and without thinking, Tem grabbed her firmly, pulling her close. He pressed his lips against hers, unleashing all his harbored feelings for her in one wet, tear-ridden kiss. As he pulled away, her eyes were wide, and the pale in her face had turned to pink.

"Remember me!" she cried as the guards pulled him away.

Chapter Three

FIVE YEARS LATER

Wake, Sizaal.

Sizaal recognized Arlac's voice booming in his mind.

"Yes, guardstone." He opened his amber eyes, adjusting them in the sunlight. By his best guess, he'd been sleeping for at least a year, siphoning power from the elements to fill his hearts.

He stood and shook off the dirt and stray plants that grew all over the branches, rocks, and roots that made up his body.

"What has happened during my slumber?" he asked, looking down from his perch to the jungle below. It stretched for miles and miles in every direction, reaching out until it touched the sea. A stream trickled nearby, and in the distance he heard the raging waterfall it would become.

A scent brought by the wind caught his attention.

"Hmm." He looked to the north, past the stream, the rocky bluffs, the sandy Deadlands, and even the wild forest. "I see… so the transformation has begun!"

He commanded the power from his wind heart, and leapt hundreds of feet into the air, riding the winds down to the jungle floor. His earth heart masked his presence, making him almost invisible as he traversed through the trees.

"It will take time," he told himself, "but all good plans do."

*****

Neema hadn't been to Essence City in over a year, but it hadn't changed. It never did. Rain sprinkled the windshield, and the night was lit by the glowing neon in Element Alley.

"Here's as good a place as any," her driver said.

"Thanks, Weex," she said, slipping him some coins. "I owe ya one."

"Don't mention it, miss," he replied. "The rebellion's always had my support. Be safe out there."

She left without another word, walking up to Element Alley, Essence City's haven for the wicked. Her breath formed in wisps in front of her, so she zipped her leather jacket tight and joined in with the crowd, hoping to keep a low profile.

One man shook a silver coin at her, but frowned when she walked away. *It's your lucky day, creep.* The last time she was here another man offered her a bronze and ended up with a black eye, dislocated shoulder, and empty purse. Neema almost gagged on the heavy stench of perversion that hung in the air.

The alley was filled with people looking for an escape, whether it be fun, drink, or pleasure. Neema couldn't blame them, but she was here for something else.

Ugh, hate this place.

She looked over to the two guards posted at each side of the alley. Guard was a loose definition for them. They were more like glorified babysitters, except they only babysat the entrance to Element Alley and occasionally broke up fights that erupted at bars. *They shouldn't be a problem.*

Neema stopped and sat at an empty bench outside of a dance club, drowning herself in the dull, pumping bass and flashing purples and greens that escaped far enough to reach her.

"I hate meeting here, you know that," Neema said.

The woman behind her remained in the shadows and sighed. "It's the only place in Essence City that gives us enough cover to do what we need. *You* know that."

"It doesn't mean I have to like it."

Neema sat for a minute in silence. She waited for a small group of young men to pass by and enter the dance club. She pitied them and envied them at the same time. The mixture of emotions only aggravated her. Those boys were lucky enough to escape forced recruitment to the mindless army, but unfortunate enough to be stuck working long hours at the stone refineries.

"So what've you got for me, Mezzy?"

Mezzy was her direct superior within the rebellion. Neema only knew she reported to Mezzy, who reported to her boss, and so on until it reached the small group that started the rebellion. Neema stuck with calling Mezzy by name.

"Strictly recon, intel, and possible recovery. *Don't* engage." Neema couldn't help but notice the emphasis on that last part. A folder slid up from a crack in the bench next to Neema. A box slid beneath the bench, hitting her foot. "There is information the council needs, and you have the resources to get it. Your briefing is in there, plus a few required tools in the box. Stay safe."

Neema knew that Mezzy was already gone. She grabbed the folder and glanced inside. There was a meeting that night between some of the king's advisers. It was assumed they would discuss information on the army's whereabouts, and knowing that would help protect the rebellion. She snapped the folder shut and sat on the bench for a few seconds longer.

"More of the same," she said, sighing. "Running, running, running. Always running."

Why can't we ever do something important*?*

It rained harder when Neema got up, and she groaned. She had gotten used to the sunshine and blue skies where the rebellion was located; a remote grouping of beaches way up north out of the mindless army's reach. She flipped up the hood of her cloak and disappeared into the crowd of Element Alley.

The meeting would be held at a private club called Teardrops in the nice part of town, near the palace. Neema knew the place. It was a dolled up version of everything Element Alley offered, so Neema's stomach churned. She knew a waitress there, so at least she'd have an in.

She tucked the file and box of tools in her pack and hopped on the motor bus. Aside from a taxi, the motor busses were the only way to get around. The driver glanced at her forged identification document and nodded. Not one set of eyes paid her any mind.

Everyone's so caught up with working themselves to death to care about little, old me.

The bus was half full, with most of the crowd in the front, so Neema took the entire back row and checked her pack. She had her two elemental rods in a separate fold, the mission briefing file, and the box of mission tools Mezzy had given her. Neema popped open the box and scowled when she saw what was inside.

A place like Teardrops required a nicer outfit than her pants, shirt, and leather jacket. Inside the box was a dress, pair of high-heeled shoes, and a small clutch. No one on the bus looked back at her, and it was dark enough inside, so she took off her shirt and slipped the dress on, unbuttoned and slid off her pants, then tossed on the heels.

The dress was cut shorter than Neema liked, both in the length and the neckline. It was a soft red number with thin straps. She adjusted herself as best she could and took out the clutch. Inside was a mirror and lipstick.

Mezzy's gotta be laughing her ass off right now. Neema shook her head and applied the lipstick. *How does anyone have time for this? It must be nice to be in the king's favor and play dress up, while all the rest of us toil away, getting run through the mud day in and day out.*

She checked her hair in the mirror, running her fingers through it and shaking it out. Then she ran her hands down her dress, smoothing it out and making sure it looked okay. It was too uncomfortable, and she had to keep her legs crossed, but she would deal with it. If she appeared awkward in it she'd lose any chance of succeeding in her mission.

Just focus, girl, she told herself. *You got this!* She took a few deep breaths to calm her nerves, then watched the rain collect and drip down the bus window until her stop approached.

A few eyes perked up as she left the bus, and the driver did a double take when she stepped down onto the curb. No doubt he wondered where she came from now that she looked like a pretty, little rich girl that didn't belong.

Teardrops was a couple blocks away, so Neema took the long way to end up at the back entrance, careful to not get her heels dirty in the muck and grime that covered the alleyways. She tapped on the door. It took almost a minute, but the latch unlocked and the dirty face of an overweight cook poked through.

"Yeah?" he asked, rubbing his running nose with his sleeve.

"Where's Donna?"

The man slammed the door, and Neema turned and waited next to the brick wall. She couldn't tell if the foul stench thick in her nostrils was from the alley, the dumpster down the way, or the cook.

Probably all three.

A few minutes later the door swung open and a spritely, young girl emerged.

"Neema, hey!"

Neema nodded and gestured to the pack she held. Donna grabbed it and looked up, her eyes as innocent as a fawn.

"I'll keep this in a safe place," Donna said. She turned to go, but paused for a moment, smushing her lips and nose together. "This won't be like that time at Lucy's is it?"

Neema smiled. Her last mission in Essence City didn't go well. "Don't worry, I'll bchave."

"Oh, good!" Donna giggled. "I like this job. The tips are great! See ya!"

The girl disappeared inside, and Neema trudged around the block to get to the front door. The line waiting to get in wrapped around the building, but Donna gave Neema exclusive access.

It's nice having a girl on the inside, Neema thought, passing everyone to the front of the line. She flashed a smile at the bouncer, who checked her name and nodded, letting her pass by.

Neema imagined the scowls of everyone in line behind her, but didn't care enough to look back. It still made her smile.

This place is actually kinda nice, she thought, crossing the club to get to the bar. People sat in their own cliques conversing, and a few couples danced, touched, and kissed to the light music played by a red-haired man with a lute. There were other outliers drinking at the bar, so Neema didn't feel as out of place.

She spotted her target at a booth in the far corner, a man named Jarrek. He was one of the king's main lackeys, coordinating the mindless army's movements.

Where are your friends, Jarrek? Neema thought. She ordered a drink, some fruity concoction a girl her age would order, and waited for the men he was meeting to arrive. It would be hard for her to listen in without making it obvious, so she sipped at her drink and turned around, thinking of ways to get closer.

Out of the corner of her eye she watched another man arrive at the table with Jarrek. *Shit!* she thought. *I'm gonna miss the entire conversation!* Perhaps she could watch and try to read their lips, but even that may draw unwanted attention.

"How about another drink?" a handsome man beside her asked, nodding to her now empty glass.

"Hmm," Neema eyed the man up and down, her lips curling into a smile. "How bout a dance instead?" She grabbed the man by the collar and pulled him to the dance floor, closer to Jarrek and his guest.

"Ooh, I like!" her date said as they started dancing. "You come here oft-"

"Shut up," she said, turning away and rubbing her backside against him.

Keeping her date occupied with her swaying hips, she listened to Jarrek and his guest talk about their drink order, Donna's nice ass, and whether they could get her into bed by the end of the night.

Assholes.

Not long after, another man joined them, but when Neema expected them all to sit down, Jarrek and the other man stood. They walked across the club, where they were escorted back to the private rooms. She cursed under her breath and turned toward her date, pulling him close.

"I have to pee." She walked off toward the bathroom, but stole a glance down the hallway the men entered. She needed to get back there, but there was a guard blocking the way.

There's gotta be another way, she thought. The bathroom didn't appear to be the way to go at first glance, but then she noticed a vent up above the mirror. *That could work.*

She locked the bathroom door, stepped up on top of the hand basin, and took the grate off the vent. A wind stone would distribute air through the vents, but it wouldn't be harsh enough to keep her from navigating them. The vent was just large enough for her to squeeze inside and shuffle around. Dirt and dust rolled along with her as she drug her elbows and knees through.

She remembered the general direction the men would be from the bathrooms, but it didn't seem like any of the shafts went that way.

"What a freakin maze," she whispered. The ventilation shafts curled, wrapped, rose, and descended, and they went everywhere except for where she needed to go! "There!" She found the end of a tunnel, so she crawled up to the grate only to find the bathroom she was just in. "Oh, you've gotta be kidding me!"

With a great deal of skill and flexibility, she slid backwards through the tunnel to find the turn she missed. After another bout of twists and turns, she thought she was going in the right direction.

Multiple vents lined the tunnel ahead, so each of those *had* to be for the private rooms. She checked the first one, but it was empty. Multiple moans and grunts carried back to her from the second room. She moved up and made sure that Jarrek wasn't a part of the sexual activities going on before she moved on to the third room.

I sure hope I'm not missing anything. She began to worry that they'd already left, but then exhaled in relief when she saw Jarrek and the others from the next vent.

"He keeps saying that this is the one he needs," one man said. "We need to bring it down, whatever the cost!"

"We won't know for sure until we kill the damned thing, and that can't be done until we dispatch more troops!" the next man said. He had a mustache and wore glasses.

Jarrek held out his hand to calm the others. "This is true. Our king is very anxious to rid himself of this plague. The mindless will take care of the beast. What concerns me at the moment is talk of this rebellion to the north."

The other two nodded in silence for a moment, then the man in the glasses smiled. "Speaking of that, I have a present for you." He walked to the door, opened it a crack, and whispered something to someone outside. A few minutes later a burly man came into the room, dragging someone draped in a hood.

"We found him sneaking around one of the mindless camps. He's part of the rebellion." Neema's mouth dropped as the captured spy fell to the floor.

The first man smiled, turning his hands amongst themselves. "Good. Leave us. Return to the palace and inform his majesty that I will return with new information shortly."

The two men nodded and left. Neema's heart began to race and her blood warmed.

"Now it's just you and me, scum," Jarrek said. His face twisted into a menacing sneer and he yanked the hood off the man. "You *will* tell me what you know."

The captive man spat blood at Jarrek's feet. "No chance in that, bub. Do your worst."

The laugh that spewed from Jarrek's mouth made Neema want to vomit. "Pride and heroics have no place in this world, *boy*. You will relinquish those qualities soon enough. Now give me the information I need. *Now*."

The captive screamed as Jarrek began torturing him, forcing Neema's eyes closed.

Someone's gotta be able to hear that, right? she thought, knowing that even if anyone did, no one would do anything about it. Just like the threesome going on next door, no one cared. Jarrek was right. This world was too twisted to allow for heroics. So why was she unscrewing the grate?

It fell with a bang, and the rest of the room went silent. Neema could almost hear the craning of Jarrek's neck as he twisted toward her. The man held captive dripped blood and one eye was red and swollen like Jarrek had merged his face with an apple. She jumped out of the ventilation shaft and expected to meet the smooth floor but felt nothing. She was suspended in midair.

Jarrek laughed. "I figured one of you rebel shit-rats would try to sabotage this meeting, though I didn't expect someone like *you*. Isn't it a school night, little girl?"

Neema tried to kick her legs, but the air around her stopped all movement. "I... What?"

"A typical reaction." Jarrek held up his hand. It glowed green.

A wind stone? But how...

"Perks of being in the king's favor," Jarrek said, like he was reading her mind. He stepped toward her, but stopped at the miniature bar and poured himself a drink. "I'd like to see what *you* know, little girl."

Neema squirmed, feeling the surrounding air press against her. He was altering enough to keep her body suspended and contained.

If I could just... She struggled, trying to stretch out as far as she could. Jarrek downed his drink in one gulp and closed in, wreaking of alcohol, sweat, and blood.

The sneering man reached out with his wind hand, "Now we play..."

There! In an instant, Neema scrunched up into a ball, creating space between her and the air Jarrek altered. She kicked, hard, against the wall of air he built. It was enough force to break through, barreling into Jarrek.

They tumbled to the ground, and Neema kept rolling, springing to her feet when she reached the bar. As she did, something about the room changed. The air *shifted.*

I gotta be quick! She reached over the counter, hoping to find what she was looking for.

"You will pay for that, li-" Jarrek started to say. Neema cut off his sentence with a match and the remaining bottle of booze, chucking it at him like a makeshift bottle bomb. Fire did wonders against wind. The flash of light blinded Neema for a moment, but she felt through the air for Jarrek's captive.

"Let's go!" she yelled. They made it out the door and down the hall, shoving everyone close by out of the way. She heard Jarrek yelling behind her, so she rushed the other rebel toward the kitchens.

Neema made eye contact with Donna from across the club, nodding to her. Donna's expression switched from excited to annoyed and then back to excited in a split second.

Just like Lucy's!

When Neema made it to the kitchen doorway, Donna already had her pack in hand ready to exchange. Neema reached out and just got her fingers on the strap when a burst of wind shot at her from behind. Her, Donna, the pack, and the poor captive, among others in the crowd, flew across the room. Neema crashed against a wall, her shoulder smashing against it with a crack. Wind flew around the room, clearing the space between Neema and Jarrek.

The smile on his face turned her stomach. "We're not done playing together, *pet*," he said.

She tried to scramble for her pack, but searing blades of wind ripped at her, tearing her dress, hair, and flesh.

"Ah!" she cried out, trying to reach her pack. *He'll rip me to pieces before I make it.*

Shattered glass rang through the club, and Neema looked up to see Donna standing behind Jarrek with a broken bottle in hand, alcohol running down his body, mixing with sweat and blood. It pooled on the floor with the shards of shattered glass.

It was enough of a distraction to give Neema time to grab her elemental rods. Across the room, Jarrek smacked Donna against the wall, then turned his attention back to Neema.

"You're gonna pay for that!" she yelled, activating the fire stone in both short staffs. Swirling flames whipped and cracked around each end, and Donna's scream echoed in Neema's mind. She lunged toward Jarrek, spit flying from between her gritted teeth.

He launched multiple blades of cutting wind, but her flames licked away every attack. Through the fire she saw a sense of urgency in Jarrek, and he hurled larger wind blades, but Neema batted each one away like it was all for sport.

"Arghh!" he growled. "You can't!"

"Watch me," she replied, dancing closer and closer in the flames toward him.

"No!" he yelled. "You will *not-*"

Neema didn't let him finish. She hurled one final fireball straight at his head, and the man dropped to the floor with a sizzling thud. She took in the sight of Jarrek's smoldering face, her fingers trembling, not from fear, but from the ecstasy the fight brought her. It wasn't the fight that thrilled her. It was the purpose. This man was a monster and had done unspeakable things to people. *Good* people. All in the name of a king who decided this was how his subjects should live. In fear.

She stood over his body. "I'm no one's pet," she said, panting hard as the adrenaline pumping within her ran its course.

The surrounding sounds began to return. The crumbling of broken tables and moaning of the injured. *Donna!* Neema ran to the young girl, lying in a heap against the wall. Neema wiped a trickle of warm blood from a cut on her face and examined her.

"Ughh…" Donna groaned. Her eyes flickered back to life and focused on Neema, slicking back her rich, smokey hair behind her ear. "I didn't think you could top Lucy's."

Neema choked out a laugh and gave Donna a hug. "Gonna have to find you a new place with tips just as good, huh?"

Donna crinkled her nose. "Eh, don't worry about it. All the guys here were assholes anyway, wasn't worth it." She gestured toward where Jarrek was piled in the middle of the club. "I'm sure he deserved what he got." Donna's eyes scanned the room, then she spoke in a hushed tone. "You better get outta here. I'll play cover up."

Neema nodded, then turned to where the rebel captive sat up against the wall, watching her with his good eye. She jogged over and helped him to his feet. "Let's go, come on."

He nodded and spat blood off to the side. "Name's Braden."

She wrapped his arm around her, shouldering some of his weight, and they walked out of the club, passing through the crowd, debris, and smoke. "I'm Neema."

By Antonio Baldari

*****

Neema pulled the blinds and let her eyes adjust to Essence City's gray, morning glow. She frowned at the view from the rebel safe house. The sparkling, gem-filled palace walls towered above the other buildings, a disdainful reminder that the king ruled over all. She searched for the sun's silhouette in the clouds, finding it an hour later than she thought.

"What a night, huh?" Braden said. He limped from the other room wearing only a towel.

Neema looked up and frowned. "Put some clothes on," she said. The swelling around his eye had gone down, but with it he donned multiple cuts and bruises down his chest and arms. Even with the injuries, there was an arrogant swagger about him, from the pretty stubble on his chin to the way he styled up his blonde hair.

"You know I never got to thank you for saving my ass back there, love," he said, tucking his thumb in the towel.

"We're leaving." She walked past him and turned, cocking her head. "And don't call me that." She grabbed her leather jacket and tied it around her waist, then pulled her hair into a ponytail.

Vendors lined the street outside of the apartment, the smells of meats and spices mixing with the city's usual stench. The market was blocks away, but in recent years it had extended out to all the side streets. Those that didn't work in the factories, and some that did, had to make a living, so more and more ended up selling whatever they could at all hours.

Neema walked down to the corner and ordered a couple pastries while she waited for Braden. They had bits of chocolate intertwined with the bread. *One of the few good things about Essence City,* she thought. She tipped the vendor, then intercepted Braden as he sauntered out of the apartment.

His eyes lowered to the pastry, smiling. "Ooh, breakfast!"

Neema scoffed. "Not for you." She pulled it out of his reach. "Keep movin!"

Neema found Mezzy waiting for them at a bench beneath a tree outside of the markets. She finished her pastry and licked the sweet, melty chocolate from her fingers, then sat next to Mezzy.

"Want it?" she asked, offering the other pastry to Mezzy.

"I don't like chocolate."

Neema cringed. "I always knew something was wrong with you."

Braden licked his lips and eyed the pastry again, but Neema shook her head and bit into it. The pastry crunched, and flakes of it fell on her lap.

"Mmm," Neema's eyes rolled to the back of her head. Mezzy frowned at her. "Oh come on! That guy had it coming, and he was crazy powerful."

"Tell me what happened. Both of you."

Neema and Braden replayed the events from the night before. Neema included the part about Jarrek being able to harness an element without losing his mind. Mezzy narrowed her eyes, but didn't appear as interested as Neema did. Had she lost no one in the mindless draft? When Mezzy was caught up, she leaned back on the bench.

"You've put us in a bad situation, Neema, and things were already bad enough."

"What's that supposed to mean?"

"Scouts say an entire mindless legion left the city this morning."

Neema took that in. "A yurdrak? Or…"

"I don't know, but we need to monitor the situation."

"And…"

Mezzy sighed. "I'm putting you on patrol back at camp."

"And what about my work here in the city!?"

"*Our* work here is over. We're too compromised."

"But-"

Mezzy held up a hand, cutting Neema's response short. "We leave now." Mezzy looked up at Braden. "All of us. There's an airship outbound tonight that will take all Essence City agents back to camp."

"Outbound from where?" Braden asked.

"It's a ways out of the city, which is why we need to leave now."

Neema's time in Essence City was cut short, again. She wished she could see her parents. *It's too dangerous to be around me, anyway,* she thought. *The further the better.* The hole in her chest would have to be filled another time.

They left Essence City within the hour. One of the shop owners near the edge of town built a tunnel that exited at the edges of the crops. As long as they watched for mindless patrols it was an easy getaway to the jungle thickets.

"So, ladies," Braden started to say, "how about we-"

"Shut it!" Mezzy and Neema commanded at once.

They travelled the rest of the way in silence aside from the rustling leaves and far off trickling brook. Mezzy led the way, her chin length, coppery red hair a beacon, seeming intent on staying distant. *Now that I think about it, I don't know her at all.* They'd been working together since Neema joined the rebellion, but all Neema knew was that she kept things short and to the point. *I like that.*

Neema watched Mezzy move through the brush. *She can't be more than five years older than I am,* she thought. Mezzy kept a lean and athletic build, but she spotted a few softer areas around her midsection, thighs, and backside.

Essence City stood behind them in the distance. The stone refineries billowed smoke, lending to the eeriness caused by the dim city lights and gray clouds above. Neema breathed in fresh air once they were far enough to see the sun break through the cloud cover.

"Not much longer," Mezzy called back, but it was hours of more walking before they made it to the rendezvous point. The sun was dipping beneath the horizon when Neema spotted the airship nestled in a clearing surrounded by boulders. She looked out past the airship to where the waves broke and crashed upon the shore, the salty breeze caressing her arms and chest.

"That thing is huge," Braden said, his eyes on the airship.

Neema nodded. It was at least five times the size of the airship she made with Tem years ago.

A crowd was at the loading deck, waiting to board, so Mezzy directed Neema and Braden to join them. Neema watched as Mezzy trailed off to speak with whom she assumed was the pilot.

"Ever been in one of these?" Braden asked. "If you get scared, you can hold my hand. There's nothing to worry about, love."

Neema huffed and glared at him until he shuffled away and interrupted a conversation others were having. A piece of the airship's rotors caught her eye, so she stalked off on her own to the wing. The ship's craftsmanship was remarkable. It would have taken her and Tem at least a decade to build something similar. Each wing had a massive rotor system attached.

"How many power stones would it take to run this?" Neema muttered to herself, her hand running along the rough metal.

"Not as many as you'd think," Mezzy said from behind her. "It's mostly powered by other things."

"Other things?" Neema asked.

Mezzy shrugged her shoulders. "Gasses or fuels or something. Oh, and no, you can't fly it. I've seen what happens when you fly."

Neema scoffed, recalling her escape from Essence City, "Did you see what I was flying? Only a true, master pilot could've taken that thing as far as I did."

"Yeah, well," Mezzy said. "Come on, we're about to lift off."

Neema gave the airship a pat, but as she looked back her focus shifted to movement out in the shadowy forest hills.

"Mez," Neema cautioned.

She heard the snarls as if the wind carried them, and Mezzy nodded, stirring to action. A group of draks took shape, barreling toward them.

"Go! Go! Go!" Mezzy shouted. "Everyone on board!"

"We'll never lift off!" Neema yelled as the rotors spurred to life. "I'll hold them!" She grabbed the elemental rods from her pack and adjusted the elements.

Lightning and wind'll work best for draks, Neema thought.

"I'll help," a man behind her said. It was getting harder to see in the setting sun, but he had a neat black beard, salted with gray hair.

"What's your name?" Neema nodded to him.

"Milo," he said. His voice was gruff and to the point.

"I like you, Milo. Let's get to work." Milo nodded and put on a pair of gauntlets. He pounded his fists together and energy crackled between them.

Neema nodded to the gauntlets, "Pretty neat. You make those?"

Milo shook his head, "Nope." He took off in a jog toward the wave of draks rising to them.

"Get that ship in the air, Mez!" Neema called out. Mezzy yelled something back, probably a lecture of some sort, but Neema was already running to catch up to Milo. Her lightning rod sparked purple, and her wind rod warped into a green glow. The draks rushing her were close enough that she could make out their bulging muscles, whipping tails, and yellow, reflecting eyes. They were like miniature versions of the larger yurdraks that terrorized the city, but without elemental powers. *Doesn't make them any less dangerous*, Neema noted, spotting the large fangs protruding from their mouths.

Milo hit first, jumping up and slamming his fists down, flattening one against the ground. It didn't even have time to yelp, and then he was rushing to the next. By the time Neema caught up several of them had surrounded him.

She swung back and blew half of them away with her wind rod, then launched a bolt of lightning at the next nearest one. The lightning flashed in the spreading shadows and over a dozen eyes glowed ahead of her. One pounced, but she knocked it away. Lightning bolts and crackling energy lit up the open field. She turned in time to see Milo knock one drak to the ground that tried to come up her flank. Neema double tapped it with another blast.

The two stood back to back, fending off the surrounding creatures with equal ferocity. Wind gusted from above, and Neema looked up to see the looming silhouette of the airship. "Milo!" Neema called out. The deafening roar of the propellers drowned out her voice, so she reached back and smacked his shoulder. "Our ride's here!" She pointed up.

He pounded his fist into a drak's face, then grunted in reply. Neema used one last blast from her wind rod to push back the remaining draks and ran for the airship. Successive pops echoed, and a drak skidded to a dead stop in front of her. Neema looked up to see someone in the loading deck of the airship with a rifle. The airship lowered down and Neema used the carcass as a lift and burst up toward it with outstretched arms.

I don't think I'm gonna make it! she thought, judging the distance in her head. If she fell back down, the horde of draks would be upon her in seconds, and she wouldn't last much longer after that. A hand reached over the airship ledge and wrapped around her own, pulling her into the craft. She rolled away from the edge, then looked up to see Braden above her, smiling casually.

"Thought you might need a hand," he said, "seein as I owe you one."

He winked at her and reached his hand out to help her to her feet.

Ew, Neema thought. She shoved his hand aside and stood on her own, rocking along with the airship's movement. Milo was already inside, tending to the cuts on his chest and arms. They made eye contact and nodded to each other, then Neema shoved Braden away and moved over to the man with the rifle.

"That was some good shooting, thanks." Neema held out her hand. "I'm Neema."

"No prob," the young man said, grabbing her hand and kissing it, though his lips only touched his thumb.

Interesting, Neema thought.

"I'm Evan."

As Evan walked away, Neema noticed a young woman leaning against the wall, staring at her while she sharpened a sword. When Neema met her gaze, the woman's face twitched and contorted. Perhaps a nervous tick of some sort?

Neema left the cargo hold and opened the cabin door, plopping down in an open seat next to Mezzy.

"You know, you're not allowed up here." Mezzy said.

"What are you gonna do, Mez? Kick me off your ship?"

"Don't tempt me." She twirled a strand of hair around her finger. "Now what do you want? I can't get you taken off patrol. It's above my pay grade."

"I want to pick my team," Neema said, pausing for a moment. "Wait, you get paid!?"

"Pick your team, huh?" Mezzy smiled. "And who are you wanting on this dream team of yours?"

"Can we skip back to the part where you get paid, and I don't?"

Mezzy tilted her head and met Neema's eyes.

"Fine, but I want Milo, and that other guy, Evan."

Mezzy leaned back in her seat and swung a leg up over the armrest. "Those two are hot. I wonder why you'd wanna work with them..." Mezzy laughed.

Neema returned the same snide look Mezzy gave her a second ago.

"Okay! Jeez. Milo doesn't play like that, anyway. I'll give them to you, but only..."

"What!?"

"Only if you take Evan's sister too. Her name's Jessii. The sexy one with the sword."

"Yeah, sure."

"And..." Mezzy smiled again. "Braden."

Neema groaned.

"It's my last offer. Take it or leave it, but if you leave it you're still stuck with Braden."

Neema stood and looked down at Mezzy. "I'll take it."

Chapter Four

"So, patrol, huh?" Braden asked. "Can't say I'm surprised. All of us aren't exactly winning medals for the rebellion."

"Speak for yourself," Evan groaned.

"Can't wait to work underneath you though, love," Braden said, turning back to Neema and grasping the rail above her.

"I'm sure I told you to stop calling me that," Neema replied, shifting out of his vicinity. He saluted in return, and Neema shook her head. "How bout you two?" she asked Milo and Jessii. "Any problems?"

They both shook their heads, but Neema noticed it looked like Jessii wanted to say something.

"What is it?" she asked.

Evan stepped in before Jessii could speak. "There's something you should know, you know, as our squad leader and all." He jutted an elbow toward Jessii. "She doesn't speak in the *traditional* sense, so it might be difficult for you to communicate. I can help translate though."

Neema nodded, thinking, but Jessii didn't appear bothered or hindered by it. "Works for me. You both have gotten this far."

Evan straightened and lowered his tone. "And ya know, we've heard a few stories about you. Pretty badass if you ask me!"

"I didn't."

"In any case, if you wanna go hunting for some bigger fish than anything we'd find on patrol, we're down!"

Neema looked Evan over. He was eager, she'd give him that, and had to be around her own age, maybe a year younger. With his neat, tidy hair, toned arms, and his open vest revealing abdominal muscles she wasn't aware existed, he was just what the rebellion wanted. A young go-getter.

Just gotta keep that fire under control, she told herself.

"We're not doing anything except for what we're told," she said, not believing she uttered those words herself. "So we patrol. Keep an eye out for draks, mindless, and anything worse. Report back if we find anything. Staying safe is what matters."

Evan appeared to deflate, but nodded and joined his sister.

As long as I stay under the radar for a little while, then maybe they'll take me off patrol and back to where things matter!

"Let's go," Neema said, bracing herself during the ship's bumpy landing.

"Barracks and tents are on the other side of camp!" Mezzy shouted as they debarked. "Grab your shit and find a bunk!"

Most of the others rushed through camp, but Neema walked casually, setting the pace for the rest of her new squad. She walked side by side with Jessii, giving Neema the chance to check her out. She and Evan didn't look much alike, but Evan claimed they were twins. Jessii kept her hair past her shoulders and shaved on one side.

"We should hurry, right?" Evan asked. "There might not be any bunks left by the time we get there!"

Neema didn't respond. Instead, she kept looking ahead and

maintained the same pace.

Gotta find a good spot, she thought. *I'll have to keep all of us together too.* Most of the dorms were large tents, but there were a couple cabins set up on the far end. Neema picked the best looking one and walked right up to it.

Inside, a group of men had just begun unpacking their things, but Neema didn't recognize them from the airship. She walked up to one bunk she liked by the window and set down her pack, right next to one of the men.

"Well lookie here, boys!" the man said. "Girlie wants to bunk with me!"

Neema twisted her lips into a frown. "Sorry, but we need this cabin. You can pack your stuff and grab a tent."

The man bellowed with laughter, his belly bouncing up and down like a mound of jelly. "That's not how it works, missy." He took a step closer to Neema, looking down at her and filling her nose with his corn chip breath. "The only way you're gettin in this bunk is if yer on top of me with those nice little legs spread. Ya feel me?" He looked to his buddies and laughed again, then reached for Neema's hips. "Now why don't you go ahead and-"

Before he could put his filthy hands on her, she plunged two fingers into the fleshy, hollow notch between his collarbones and yanked down.

"Kahhh!" he squawked.

"Now listen here," Neema whispered, spinning around and using the man's weight to guide him face first into the wall. She curled his wrist up, keeping a firm grip on his thumb. "You and your *boys* are gonna move on over to the tents, while I'm still asking nicely. Got it?" For added emphasis, she dug her knee up between the man's legs, squishing his manhood between her knee and a hard place.

"Now, Neema…" Braden interjected. "Maybe-"

"Did you say Neema?" the man pinned against the wall asked, his voice a pitch higher than before. "Like, *that* Neema that tore up Lucy's club last year!?"

They always have to bring up Lucy's…

She pressed against him so her lips were an inch from his ear. "Why don't you stick around and find out?"

"I'm leavin," one of the other men said, and the others followed suit.

"Cabin's yers," the man she held grunted.

"Why thank you," Neema said, shoving him aside so he could grab his things and leave.

She plopped backwards onto the mattress. "Pick your bunks, squad."

"Well if it's alright with you," Braden said, reaching for the bunk above hers.

Neema stuck out her foot, holding him in place. "It's not. Over there." She pointed across the room.

As if she knew what Neema would suggest, Jessii tossed her bag on the top bunk and hopped up, half smiling at Neema as she did.

Braden walked to the next bunk, but Neema stopped him again. "Nope. Keep going. That one there, on the other side of the room. Yep."

"Was it something I said?" Braden muttered, setting his pack down and leaning back on his bunk, out of sight from Neema's current position.

Well that's a little better, she thought, smiling and turning to look out the open window. She could make out the bluffs in the distance that overlooked the ocean.

"Take the rest of the day to do whatever you need to," she said, closing her eyes. "We're on patrol bright and early tomorrow."

Neema laid down for a while before getting up and stretching. The others left, so she strolled around camp. It changed little since the last time she was there, so she didn't bother walking around to check it out. She knew where the baths, armory, and headquarters were. All were makeshift tents or cabins not meant to last long. At least they were far enough out of the king's reach to stay safe. That's why patrolling was so important, even if it was grueling.

Mezzy, you better not make me do this grunt work for long, Neema thought, walking out of camp to get a better look at the bluffs she saw from her window. *And leading this group. That'll be a challenge on its own.*

She noticed a tiny path leading up through them, and water splashed in the distance, echoing off the rock walls.

"Seems interesting," she said, wondering what might be up there.

Her grumbling belly interrupted her curiosity, so she turned back to camp. *I suppose exploring can wait*, she thought. *Better eat and rest while I still can.*

*****

"Load up!" Neema called. They'd been patrolling for weeks and found nothing at all. It was like time crawled by, especially with Braden annoying her, Milo keeping his distance, Jessii being weird and silent, and Evan kissing her ass every step of the way.

Gotta do it though, she thought.

"Jungle route again?" Braden complained. "Ugh!"

Neema didn't bother responding. She grabbed her pack and led the group east out of camp and into the deep part of the jungle. It was a mess of thick trees, strange plants, and even stranger wildlife. Most animals didn't bother them and would scurry away as they approached. The sun shone down through gaps in the canopy above, but only in patches. Still, Neema enjoyed peeking up at the clear skies. She remembered Essence City was always cloudy. If only her parents could see the blue skies her mother dreamed about. She regretted leaving the city at times. It had been over two years since they refused to join her escape.

Don't worry, Neema thought. *I'll come back and end the king's reign. For the both of you. And for Tem.*

"Why don't we just saunter along and find something better to do with our time?" Braden said. "We could kill a few hours and head back to camp. There's never anything out here any-"

"Shh!" Neema hushed, noticing something up ahead.

"What, no-"

"Shut. Up." Neema raised a hand, intensifying her stare, and Braden picked up the hint.

Neema lowered her head and looked across the clearing. Really looked.

"When was the last time we were on this route?" Neema asked.

"Late last week," Evan replied. "What is it?"

"I don't remember that." She pointed up ahead, where a tree and the surrounding ground had been scorched, blackened, and burned. She sat on a rock and stared at the charred ground, trying to come up with anything else that may have caused it.

"How did that happen?" Evan whispered.

"I have a guess," Neema said.

Evan smiled, "You don't think…" His smile faded. "You're kidding."

"Shouldn't we turn back?" Braden asked. "Come back with a full contingent?"

Neema shook her head. "We're patrol. We must assess the threat, and we're too far from camp. By the time we make it there and back it may be too late."

Evan loaded a clip of water bullets in his rifle. Milo was ready with his elemental gauntlets, and Jessii wrapped her hand around the hilt of her sword.

"We pursue." Neema smiled. "You wanted some action, right?"

"I'd rather have some milder action than chasing a blasted yurdrak," Braden said. "You know, maybe a stray mindless wandering around, a couple of small draks, some rebelling rebels to spar with." He stretched his limbs and slipped two long knives from each sleeve of his cloak.

"Can't be too picky." Neema nodded to the scorched earth, and they started to track. The burns didn't look more than a week old, and that was the last time they patrolled this route. It was a good thing they didn't cross paths directly. Coming up over a ridge onto a yurdrak is not how Neema wanted to spend an afternoon.

Now we become the hunter.

It didn't take long to pick up the yurdrak's trail. Every hundred yards they'd find charred clearings.

"Each of these spots are most likely footprints," Milo said, rubbing his hand along the burned remains of a group of trees. "It's amazing that it doesn't leave more of a trace than this."

"Makes it hard to track," Braden said, and for once Neema agreed with him.

"It's probably halfway across the country by now," Evan said.

"What do you think the mindless army does out here?" Neema asked. "They've been chasing this thing in circles all these years, wasting those boys' lives." *Boys like Tem.*

Neema hadn't thought about him much over the years. Whenever her thoughts drifted back to him she shook them away, burying them further and further. All she could allow was to promise that someday she would end the use of the mindless and bring him back to her. If he was even still alive.

Perhaps Evan's right, she thought, trying to forget Tem again. "I don't think we're gonna find any-"

A twig snapped nearby, and everyone stopped in their tracks. Neema nodded to Evan, and he signaled to Jessii. Her smaller build made her the better scout. She dashed toward the source of the noise, moving as silent as her shadow.

The quiet, young woman, wearing short shorts and a crop top, climbed up a tree and crouched, peering over a branch like a monkey. After a moment, she signaled back to them.

"Just a jungle churoki," Evan said.

"How do you even know what she's communicating, mate?" Braden asked.

"Have I not told you that we're twins?"

Braden scoffed. "That doesn't give you special powers!"

Neema ignored the rest of the conversation and moved up with Milo. The small churoki huddled against a tree, its big ears moving back and forth. Once Braden and Evan appeared, it raised the courage to sprint off in the brush.

Neema looked around at the thick leaves and crawling plants on the forest floor. There were no signs of fire here. Did they get turned around? Neema spun in each direction. She was sure the tracks of flames led this way.

Maybe it's time to head back, she thought.

Then Jessii whistled.

Neema followed the direction she was facing and hopped on top of a boulder to give herself a better view. In front of her, a valley lay in between her and a mountain. Torched, black tracks led down to a huge hole in the middle of the valley. All Neema could see within was a deep, mysterious black.

"Let's check it out," she said, and they made their way down the valley toward the wide, gaping hole. As they approached, she noticed something strange about the burn marks that led within the earth.

Are those rocks melted? It's like the mountain got all sweaty and poured rock all over the valley. Neema knew firsthand how hot a yurdrak's fire was, but hot enough to melt rock? Was that possible?

Milo grabbed a rope from his pack and secured it to a tree.

"Give it here." She motioned for the rope, wanting to be the first to descend. She grabbed one of her elemental rods, switched to fire, to help light her way. The further Milo lowered her down the warmer the cavern got.

That's strange, she thought. *It's supposed to be colder down here.* The others followed, but aside from the noise they made it was quiet. *The yurdrak wouldn't still be inside. Would it?*

Milo cracked open a few glow sticks and tossed them around to the others. The cavern was huge, and appeared empty. Darker and darker it got until what little light from the hole they climbed into was nonexistent. The path snaked beneath the forest, and the deeper it led them the more Neema was sweating from the heat.

"You know, love, if we come face to face with that beast then there's no way we'll get outta here alive," Braden whispered.

Neema turned and leveled her eyes at him. "Don't tell me you're scared. You of all people?"

"Of course I'm scared. I've heard what those things can do."

"Have you ever seen one, Braden?"

"No."

"I've seen this beast up close. It's because of it that I'm even here and not still stuck in Essence City."

"So you kinda owe it a favor then, ya?"

Neema didn't answer.

"What happened?" Evan asked.

Neema didn't answer that either.

Milo rounded the next corner and jolted to a stop, Jessii too. Neema caught up and saw why. Her heart launched up to her throat, stopping her breath. It was the yurdrak. It was lying on the ground, facing them. She remembered almost exactly what the yurdrak looked like when it attacked Essence City five years ago, but something about it was different. It looked... dead.

Neema walked up to it, it was still hot enough to turn the entire cavern into a furnace, but it was like it had lost its fire. Then she walked around it and saw why.

"Oh my," she said. It was dead, but in such a terrible way. The head was mostly intact, but at the neck its skin was ripped and cracked to pieces. The body was largely whole, but the limbs were in fragments too. It was like something killed it from the inside, and came out, like-

"It's a shell," Milo said.

Jessii raised an eyebrow at Milo's assessment.

"Oh, don't look so surprised," he said. "I studied biology before that broken system forced me to work in the factories."

"Look at the way the skin is cracked," Evan added, "and over there, what's that?" He pointed to the other side of the cavern.

Neema brought out her other fire rod, splashing the cave in orange light. What Evan saw was a broken chrysalis.

"Did it… transform?" Milo asked. "Some type of metamorphosis maybe."

"But how? And what did it turn into?" Neema asked. No one answered, and for that she was grateful. She followed the cavern past the chrysalis and scorched markings on the cavern walls toward a dim light. It led upwards, tunneling until it opened to a vast hole in the mountain's side.

She stood at the edge with Milo and the others beside her, looking out at the land stretched out before them. The mountain dove toward the rocky shore where waves crashed and churned. The coast met with the forest, creating a mess of boulders and sharp, spiky ledges hidden amongst the trees.

That would be messy, Neema thought, taking a step back. She noticed Milo fade behind the others, keeping clear of the edge altogether.

"Check that out," Evan said, pointing to charred scarring in the mountainside that led into the forest before disappearing. "I hope that thing is as far away as possible."

The sun began to set, lighting the mountains in the distance like they were ablaze. A chilling wind blew in, reminding Neema that nighttime was almost upon them. "Let's set up camp. We'll stay in here tonight."

"Well it is pretty warm," Braden said. "You know-"

"Not another word," Neema said, cutting him off before he finished whatever crude remark he was about to make.

Sleep only lasted a few hours. She rolled back and forth on the terribly uncomfortable rock floor, searching for that sweet spot that remained hidden. That, and the unsettling, overbearing reality that the yurdrak was here not even a few days ago weighed down on her, keeping her awake. She peered out to the night sky outside, watching the millions of stars twinkle at her until the sun washed them all away.

"Back to camp!" she called out, waking the others. "Gotta update em on what we found."

They winded their way back through the tunnels to the burrowed hole in the valley. That's when Neema heard it.

"That sounds like..." she started.

"Running water," Milo finished for her.

Evan looked confused. "I don't remember a river up there when we came down yesterday."

"Ahh shit," Braden cursed, echoing Neema's thoughts.

"Everyone back to the cavern," Neema said. "Now!" She let them get a head start, hoping the sound was something, anything, else. Mere moments later, mist and sparkling water rained down, followed by the shape of a mindless soldier surfing a wave through the hole.

Crud, she thought.

Neema backed up behind a pile of melted rock and peeked out far enough to watch another watermind drop to the floor. Then another. Soon a whole squadron was down there. She knew she should hurry and get out of there, but she wanted to see if he was there.

Tem, where are you?

She leaned forward far enough that she slipped, and her footstep echoed off every wall inside. A dozen blue eyes became alert in an instant, so Neema took off as fast as she could. It wouldn't take long for them to catch up to her, they were trained soldiers with the power of an entire element at their disposal.

As she ran, she flipped open the stone compartment on one of her elemental rods. She pulled the lightning stone out of its holster and jammed it into a stun grenade, connecting it to the trigger. She pulled the pin and tossed it behind her to where the closest watermind was gaining on her. His eyes showed no emotion until lightning reflected in them. Then they flashed fear and anger all in one. Lightning could have devastating effects on a water elemental, and she just created a lightning trap at the only tunnel opening.

That should keep you from getting in, she thought. *For a little while anyway.* If she figured it up in her mind right, the lightning stone would have enough power to keep them at bay for about a minute.

What she would do at the cavern cliff edge was another problem. Everyone in her squad depended on her. The answer evaded her with each breath and every step she ran.

What do I do!?

Milo and the others were at the cliff edge looking in every direction. Jessii clicked her lips and motioned toward a ledge along the mountainside they might use. Neema nodded. One at a time they filed onto the narrow ledge, inching their way across the mountain.

"Sure hope this doesn't drop off!" Braden said.

"You just had to say that!" Evan yelled.

As they curved along the side of the mountain, the cliff edge that led into the mountain disappeared from view. Voices shouting from the mountainside opening carried out to her. She'd never heard a mindless speak before, but she could make out the words "yurdrak," "rebels," and "find them!"

Neema tried not to look over the edge, but she had to look down to watch her foot placement. Naturally, her eyes shifted to take in the thousand foot drop to the sharp rocks below, almost causing her to bump into Milo. He kept looking over the side too, making his progress slow to a crawl. As big as he was it was harder for him to find good foot placement. The others were already around the bend up ahead, nearly out of sight.

"Gonna make it, big guy?" Neema asked.

Milo sighed. "Never been one for heights."

"You know…" Neema said, looking over the edge again. "When I was younger, a friend of mine was terrified of heights. We stole some apples from a vendor in the market and ran off to hide. One of the guards found us and chased us up the roof of a building that overlooked the bay." Neema smiled. "Tem was so scared I actually saw his knees shake. There was only one way we would get away, and that was jumping off the building. I yelled at Tem, 'Jump! It'll be okay!' He wouldn't do it. So I pulled him off the roof with me. He cried and tried to hold his footing, but I wouldn't let go. We soared through the air and splashed into the water. Then we hid underneath the docks until the sun set. Couldn't keep Tem off those damn roofs after that."

Neema realized that Milo had stopped to turn and look at her.

"What?" she asked.

"That was a nice story. It made you smile."

"I know how to smile, Milo."

"That was a *real* smile, Neema."

More shouting rose from behind her, too close to have come from the cliff edge. The waterminds were in pursuit.

"Shit! We have to go!"

Milo heard it too and moved faster. As much of an improvement as her story made on his pace, it still would not be enough. Within minutes the mindless would be upon them, and in that case they might as well be dead. Either they'd fall to their messy deaths, the mindless would kill them, or enslave them to return and face the king's judgment in Essence City. The king had never issued a favorable judgment. Ever.

"Go, Milo, get the others back to camp!"

"What are you doing?"

"I can distract them, and hopefully get them off our tail."

"It's too dangerous, Neema!"

Neema didn't have time for this. "Get back to camp, damnit! I didn't ask for your fuckin opinion!"

Milo's nostrils flared, but he nodded and kept moving along the ledge.

Neema turned and faced the other direction. She grabbed both of her elemental rods and flicked them on. One to earth, and the other to wind.

Never tried this before, she thought, hoping her half-cooked plan would pan out. Jumping out over the edge, she shot a blast from her earth rod at the side of the mountain, creating a step stone for her to jump onto. With her wind rod, she launched herself into the air, spinning and slicing both of her rods toward the side of the mountain. Once she reached the apex of her jump, she swung once more with her earth rod, sending cracks and splinters up the mountain. Then with her wind rod she shook the mountain, creating a terrible avalanche.

Boulders hurdled toward the unknowing mindless. Some of them activated their water powers to shield themselves or deflect the incoming debris, which created a mess of rocks, dirt, water, and bodies. Neema sprung from boulder to boulder, whipping down and down using both rods to clear her path.

The hulking avalanche gained on her, and even as she tried to run along the side of the mountain it gained strength, biting at her heels.

Behind her, the waterminds yelled and used their powers to protect themselves and attack her at the same time. Rushing water hit one of her footholds and it broke off, causing her to slam against the mountainside and tumble along the rocks. She tried to correct herself with each of her rods, but it was no use. Water, rocks, and dirt showered and pelted her as she neared the forest floor.

"Come on!" she yelled, swinging her wind rod to the ground to slow her descent. A shadow enveloped her in a terrible darkness. She screamed, but the thundering avalanche around her drowned out any other noise. An instant later, the back of her head exploded in pain and consciousness left.

*****

"Is that what you wanted me to see, Arlac?" Sizaal asked, not expecting an answer. It was a curious thing, what he witnessed. He stood above the woman, studying her features. "Such a fragile thing, yet she nearly brought down the entire mountain. Recklessness? Or valor?"

His thoughts returned to the muddled, confused, and dangerous creature as he finished preparing the cave. *It has been many years since a yurdrakon walked this planet. And what a dangerous combination of elements...* He shook his head and molded stone together with his earth heart like a potter would shape a bowl.

"This should be useful." He filled it with water created from his water heart, then activated his fire heart to heat it until it began to steam. After that, he lit a small fire nearby to keep her warm until she woke.

He returned to the young woman and laid his hand on her forehead. From what he sensed, her organs were intact, but she had a few broken bones. "I will give you a gift, young one." Sizaal dug deep within him, tapping what Essence he held. "This should help." The Essence flowed through him, attaching itself to her injuries. He sensed her bones reattach, her bruises clear away, and her cuts mend. In moments, color brightened her face and her breathing returned to normal. Like a switch in his mind, he cut off the flow of Essence, keeping what little remained. *I feel I will need it soon.*

With that, Sizaal bowed his head to her. "Safe journeys, little one. I expect our paths will cross again."

Chapter Five

Neema didn't understand. *I'm supposed to be dead, right?* She was in a freaking avalanche! An avalanche she caused. Plus there were a bunch of pissed off waterminds who wanted her dead.

"Woah," she said, looking around. "Where am I?"

She stood straight up, causing her head to swim. With clenched fists, she searched the cave top to bottom. "Milo!" she called out, using the cave wall as a crutch to lean on. It's unnaturally smooth walls unsettled her. "Jessii!" Only the crackling fire responded. She was alone.

What is going on!? she wondered. She leaned over the pool and let the steam warm her face, looking down at her reflection. Dirt coated her face, and her hair was a disheveled mess, but as she felt the back of her head and the rest of her body, she realized she wasn't hurt at all. All the traces of her slide down the mountain were there, the dirt and torn clothes, but no cuts, bruises, or broken bones. *How strange.*

As she breathed the pure, cave air her worries drifted away like the embers floating from the fire. It was like the cave itself was telling her that it was safe, soothing away her wariness.

"I suppose I could hang out for a bit," she said. A hint of caution remained, so she kept her elemental rods within reach as she undressed and dipped into the pool.

"Ahh," she sighed, leaning back and soaking in the heat. She washed away the dirt and blood, though she had no scars, and let the water relax her remaining tension away.

Once bathed, Neema washed her clothes and hung them over the fire to dry. She still had a bit of food in her pack, so she crunched on some jerky and cooked a few mushrooms she found growing in the cave.

"I should probably head out," Neema told herself, noticing it was getting darker outside. *Didn't realize I've been here for so long.*

She dressed and left the cave, entering the cool, evening air. The setting sun cast a thousand shadows from all the trees in the jungle, and slices of sunlight retreated to the horizon. After a few minutes of walking, Neema looked back to where the cave was, but nothing remained but rocks and dirt.

Could've sworn it was right there...

She hastened her way through the jungle, wondering why she awoke in the magical cave. *I thought whenever a woman needed saving, a gorgeous man was supposed to come save her,* she thought. *Not some stupid cave. Are strong shoulders and nice dimples too much to ask for?*

Neema kept walking, watching over her shoulder in case anyone trailed her. After about an hour she climbed up a tree to get her bearings. The mountain was to the north, and she could make out the deep scar her stunt inflicted on its side.

I did that!? she thought. "At least that yurdrak isn't around anywhere. That I can see anyway." That could be a good or bad thing as she thought about it. The dreaded monster might pop up out of nowhere and fry her with one swipe of its paw. Neema hoped her luck hadn't run out yet.

With some quick navigating, she was on her way back to camp hoping the others were safe. The surrounding jungle was quieter than usual, putting Neema on alert and slowing her pace. Beside her, only a few yards away, a twig snapped and sent her crouching behind a rock.

In the blink of an eye she jumped out with her lightning rod, crackling and flashing across the jungle floor.

"Woah, woah!" Braden jumped back and raised his arms high in the air. "It's just me, love!"

"What the hell, Braden!?" Neema said. "What are you doing out here? Why aren't you back at camp?"

"We never made it that far," Braden said.

"What happened?"

"After we made it down the mountain, a squad of waterminds was waitin for us. They weren't too happy either, after seein what you did. It sounded like you brought the whole mountain down! We thought you were dead for sure."

"So how did you guys escape?"

"Oh, *we* didn't. *I* did. Slipped my cuffs and took off when I found an opening. Been wandering out here all day." He scratched the back of his head. "Not sure which way camp is though."

Neema's mouth dropped. "Camp is the exact opposite direction that you've been going, and what the hell!? We have to go rescue the others!"

"Love, I don't think you heard me, there's a squad of waterminds, who have now most likely met up with a *legion* of waterminds. Unless you've got another mountain in that pack of yours to bring down on them, I don't think you've got a chance."

"*We*," Neema said as she looked off through the brush.

"Say again?"

Neema turned and faced Braden. "We. *We* have a chance. Not me. We're a team, so you're coming with me."

Braden grinned in a devilish fashion and tried to flash his eyebrows at Neema. "I think I should get back to camp, love. Someone's gotta report in everything we've seen!"

"We'll do that after we rescue everyone, as a team. Plus, I wouldn't want you getting lost again."

Neema turned and started to walk in the direction Braden had come from.

"You could've just pointed to which way camp was," he said, "I would've found it eventually."

Braden wasn't much help in figuring out which way the watermind camp was, but Neema found a trail to follow. They ended up reaching a good vantage point to look down at the mindless camp. Neema stayed just out of sight of the patrols, but Braden was right, it was an entire mindless legion. There were enough soldiers to invade camp and destroy the rebellion in one swoop.

"Uhh," Braden started to say.

"I know," she answered. Their odds weren't good.

The only reason the rebellion lasted so long was because it did well to stay hidden. The camp moved periodically, and it stayed far enough out of Essence City's reach. The mindless army was usually too busy chasing the yurdrak to take the time and search for the rebellion.

"This isn't good," she muttered.

"If the king sent a cursed *legion* this far north," Braden said, "he either really wants that blasted yurdrak dead, or else…"

He didn't need to finish. It could mean the king wanted to find the rebellion and snuff it out for good. Either way, the mindless army this far north was too unsettling. She needed to get her squad and get back to camp.

Braden pulled out a scope and scanned the camp.

"What do ya see?" she asked.

"There." He pointed and handed her the scope. There was a large tent set up in the middle of the camp with guards posted on either side of the entrance. "That's gotta be where they're keeping em. Kept me in a similar one back when I got caught."

"Okay, now we need a diversion," she said, thinking. "I just might have one too." She grabbed an elemental rod and pulled out its fire stone. Braden kept a spool of wire on his utility belt, and she pointed it at. "I need that." She began rigging up the wire with some power chips and detonators, then grabbed one of Braden's knives and began slicing the fire stone to pieces.

"Just take what you want," Braden said, crouching next to her. "Don't mind me." He kept his blades sharp, so she had little trouble cutting through the softer elemental stone. "Is that safe?" he asked.

Smaller pieces were ideal for the explosive she was creating. Once broken down, the stone couldn't be melded back together without going to one of the king's refineries. She flipped the knife in her hand and held it back out for him, then picked up her finished explosive.

"It's not pretty, but it'll make for quite the show." She gave one end of the spool of wire to Braden. "Okay, I'll take this out and stretch it through the jungle."

She walked the line out, making sure no mindless patrolled as far out as she went. The night was quiet, and the smell of decaying plants and rotting leaves filled the air. Neema could taste the thick humidity, knowing in a few, long moments the surrounding vegetation would be set afire. Once the line stretched as far as she could pull it, she dashed back through the jungle, breezing by and causing random drops of dew to fall from nearby leaves.

Neema shooed Braden away from the line and sent him back toward the camp. She swiped a flint onto the wire, and waited for the spark to glow orange, crawling to the first detonator. It sizzled through the quiet, but Neema could barely hear it over the thumping of her heart.

"Time to go," she told herself, taking off after Braden. Tree branches whipped by, and she kicked through tall grass with each pounding step. Ahead, Braden slowed, looking back to Neema for direction. She sliced with her arm, motioning to the outside perimeter of the camp. Braden took off again, though at a slower pace, and in a moment she passed him.

The lines exploded behind them in huge infernos. Neema felt the searing heat on her back and glanced with the corner of her eye at the towering flames. At a distance it would appear a giant fireball was rolling through the jungle, or a fire yurdrak was taking a stroll through the woods.

"Oh crap!" Braden whispered between breaths.

"That should keep them busy for a while," Neema called behind. "Let's go!"

He followed, and they circled around the camp to avoid any scouts. By the time they made it to the outside perimeter she could see the commotion within, swarming like angry wasps. There weren't any soldiers on the other side of the fence at the spot Neema wanted to climb over, so she nodded to Braden.

He shot a grapple from his wrist and pulled himself up and over, then nodded the all clear to Neema. She switched her elemental rod to wind and launched herself in the air, flying over the gate and landing on the other side next to Braden.

"You made those things?" Braden asked, nodding to her rods.

"Hm," Neema nodded.

"Quite convenient, care to make one for me?"

Neema didn't answer. It took almost a year to make them, and she wasted a dozen elemental stones in the process. It was painstaking work, but they'd saved her life many times over.

The slight breeze dug through Neema's jacket, giving her goosebumps. She rubbed her arms through her jacket, avoiding any passing mindless soldier as her and Braden snuck through the camp.

This place is huge, she thought, comparing it to the other mindless camps she'd been in. Still, everything inside had a purpose, which did *not* include pleasure.

Terrible, she thought. How could a society force its children to join something so lifeless?

They approached the detention tent, and Neema peeked around the corner at the two mindless soldiers guarding it.

"Windminds?" Neema whispered. "Why would there be other elements here?"

"Who knows?" Braden replied. "Maybe they just use em as guards or something."

Windminds would be no help in an attack against a firedrak. It would burn right through them without so much as snorting a fireball. Could it mean something else? Neema shook the thought away, hoping Braden was right. It was useless to try to figure out how the mindless operated.

"Let's take out the two guards, then you keep watch while I'm inside," she told him.

Braden nodded, and together they snuck toward the tent. Neema grabbed her elemental rods, switching one to fire and the other to lightning. She bent over like a runner preparing for a sprint, the dewy blades of grass wetting her fingers.

I'm sorry for this.

After a quick breath, she burst forward. The two guards immediately reacted, arming themselves with swirling gusts of wind, but in a dazzling bout of fire, wind, knives, and lightning, they fell.

"Rghh!" Hot blood trailed down her cheek.

"You okay?" Braden asked as he sheathed his knives.

She wiped the blood with her sleeve. "Stay here."

Neema flipped open the flap of the tent and stepped inside, taking in the dim lighting. Metal bars lined both sides of the tent, and at the far end she saw Milo, Evan, and Jessii each in separate cells.

"Figured that was you outside," Milo said. "Not much gets those mindless goin like when they see trouble, and you're *full* of trouble."

Neema smiled and looked at the locks holding them in their cells. It would take too long to cut through them with her wind rod, so she looked around for a key. Nothing.

"Alright, Evan," Neema said. "Get in the corner. I'm gonna try somethin." She switched one of her rods to earth and the other to wind.

"Oh shit, Neema," Evan said, clinging to the far wall of his cell. "Are you sure abou-"

She swung both rods at the ground in front of Evan's cell. The rods combined to push the earth beneath the cell, creating a makeshift escape tunnel.

"Ha!" Neema cried out, smiling at Evan. The ground spat dirt at him, covering him from head to toe. "Now you're free!"

She did the same for Milo and Jessii, pulverizing the ground in an explosion of dirt. As the crew grabbed their gear to leave, something echoing in the distance froze Neema in place. A scream so powerful it sounded as if it came from hell, vibrating the ground beneath her feet.

"Is that what I think it is?" Evan asked.

Neema heard that same scream five years ago. She rushed out of the tent, unsure of what she might see. The cool night air suddenly seemed a lot warmer.

"Wait, where's Braden? Braden!" she called out for him, but he was nowhere in sight. "Damnit!"

In the distance, mindless scrambled to ready themselves for an attack, and the yurdrak let out another mighty roar.

"We should get out of here, boss lady," Evan said. Neema nodded and hustled back toward where her and Braden jumped the fence.

"Does everyone have a way over?" Neema asked.

Evan and Jessii nodded, but Milo shook his head.

Right, Neema thought. *He's afraid of heights.*

"You two go! Milo and I will meet you where the river forks, about five miles northeast of here! Go!"

Neema and Milo ran along the wall toward the only opening on the perimeter, the front gate. It was dark enough to sneak in the shadows, and the mindless must have cleared out of camp to chase the yurdrak.

It almost seems too *quiet up here though,* she thought. Although, it *was* tempting to peek around the rest of the camp to see what she could find. *I wonder if there are any important officers with useful information on the king. There has to be a way of dethroning him. There has to!*

Neema slowed, taking in her surroundings. *If I were an officer where would I-*

"Neema!" Milo said. "You okay?"

"Yeah, I just gotta-"

Before she finished, a wave crashed into her, tossing her against a tent.

"Neema!" Milo yelled, his voice muffled by the water in her ears.

"Gurghh," she choked, coughing up water. She struggled to get to her feet, slipping and falling back to the ground. Through the waterlog, Milo's gauntlets buzzed and zapped as he fought the mindless. How many were there? Surely he couldn't take them all on his own.

I have to help! She scrambled to the edge of the tent, finding her elemental rods. "Rah!" she cried. Out of the corner of her eye, one soldier waited for her to get within reach. An instant before she could wrap her hands around one of her rods, he sent another water blast straight for her. This time, she rolled to the side, yanking a stake from the ground and hurling it at the soldier. That gave her just enough time to roll back and grab both rods.

She joined both rods, forming a long staff with her remaining lightning stone activated at the tip. It crackled and snapped as she swung the staff above her head. "Take this!" she yelled.

Before she could finish her sweeping strike, she stopped dead. The two waterminds in front of her waited, arms raised and ready to defend against her attack. She almost couldn't believe it, but she'd never forget that almost white hair and the way he scrunched his nose when he was confused.

It was Tem.

Chapter Six

His eyes glowed a brilliant blue, and he'd grown since Neema last saw him, but it was definitely Tem. She nearly choked on air, but somehow found her tongue.

"Tem!" she cried. "It's me, Neema! Remember?"

He didn't show any reaction, but he didn't attack either. The other mindless lurked closer, step by step.

"Neema…" Milo cautioned.

"Come on, Tem, you have to remember! Help me! Come with us!"

The other watermind reacted first, shooting a water blast at Neema. Milo jumped in front of her, intercepting it with his lightning gauntlets. Then he punched back a blast of electrocuted waves, dropping the watermind to the ground. Milo yanked Neema away, dragging her toward the front gate before the soldier recovered. Neema stole a look at Tem as they retreated. He stood tall, regarding her with those brilliant blue eyes and tensed muscles. He didn't pursue or move an inch, but she knew he was watching her.

The yurdrak screamed again, and Neema forced herself to look out into the distance. She whipped her head back around, flipping her hair against Milo's face as he led her away from camp. The camp behind them was quiet, dark, and empty, Tem disappeared into the night. In that instant, it didn't feel real at all. Was he even there? She'd waited so long to see him again, and the moment passed all too quickly.

"Tem…" she muttered to herself, tearing away from Milo and jogging on her own.

Smoke billowed off in the forest. She couldn't see the monster, but Neema knew it was out there. Tem was out there too. He was alive, and within her grasp. She could've reached out and touched him. It was too much to process.

Everyone knew mindless didn't retain any glimpses from their former life. Neema tried to tell herself that over and over, but it was like he *knew* her. The other mindless attacked her, why didn't he?

"Wanna talk about it?" Milo asked, stopping in a small clearing within a group of large boulders. He took out his pack and began rummaging through it.

"No," she replied, and started adjusting her elemental rods.

"Good," Milo said. He sat down and leaned against the rock, looking up to the sky.

"Why are we stopping?" she asked. She was down one lightning stone, a fire stone, and her wind stone needed adjusting before it could work again.

Neema realized her chest was heaving and her breath still labored. *A short break wouldn't hurt.* For a few minutes, Neema embraced and enjoyed the silence. She knew she could count on Milo not to pry.

"That was that kid you told me about, right?"

Neema glared at him until he sat back against the rock and looked back up at the stars. Neema shook her head and continued her adjustments. *Stupid wind stone.* That's when she noticed she had a cut on her lip dripping blood. She wiped it away with her hand and continued. *Great, now I'm gonna have a fat lip.*

"Because if it *was* that kid-" Milo started.

"Shut *up*, Milo."

"Now hear me out," Milo said. "What if we did something... reckless?"

"The hell are you talkin about?"

"That kid, Tem-"

"He's not a kid, he's the same age as me."

"At my age, you're all kids, girl," Milo chuckled, and Neema tried not to smile. "If we were to make contact with him, see, I've been reading through some notes I stole from this miss-, well anyway, I think I understand enough to manipulate the effects the water stone has on him."

"You can bring him back?"

Milo squinted. "I know enough that I might be able to lessen the mind controlling effects. Without knowing what the king and his researchers know, any major adjustments could kill him. The water stone is placed too close to the brain stem. His body is literally a part of the water element."

The science was lost on Neema, but what Milo said was intriguing. If he lessened the control the water stone had on Tem, then he could do it to all the mindless.

"You're pretty good at buildin stuff, right?" he asked. Neema raised an eyebrow. Milo returned a toothy grin, which was rare for him. "I might need your help with something if this is gonna work."

Neema nodded, thinking. "Why would you do this? What's it to you if a mindless is cured?"

Milo looked away for a moment, then shook his head. "Just tryin to help is all. Just tryin to help."

They sat in silence under the canopy of stars for a few more minutes before packing up to meet Evan and Jessii. A chorus of cicadas and other night pests played, and Neema welcomed the background noise as she thought about what Milo suggested.

Would we even see Tem again? she asked herself. *Would the device work?* There was so much to think about and do to implement any sort of plan. Could she even risk her squad mates on such a mission? She'd have to think about that later. First, she needed to build whatever device Milo needed. *I'll figure out the rest later.*

They reached a rough jungle thicket, and water faintly trickled in the distance. "We're getting close," Neema whispered. She pulled out her elemental rods, just in case there was a trap lying in wait up ahead. Huge plants grew in between boulders, making their trek slower than the sun peeking over the horizon. It made for a humid early morning, and Neema felt herself sweating through her clothes. *Gross.* Judging by the amount of times Milo wiped his forehead he had the same problem.

As breaking rapids appeared through a gap in the foliage, Neema felt like someone in the distance was watching them. She gripped her elemental rods tighter, ready to attack. The leaves ahead shifted, but there was no breeze to fault. Neema tilted her head, focusing.

A feint! She swung behind to her right when Jessii appeared through the thick, green brush. Neema stopped her rod short of Jessii's cheek, tossing a strand of the girl's hair in front of her unblinking eyes. Jessii's lip twitched up, and her eyes travelled down to Neema's neck. That's when Neema felt the hot sting of Jessii's blade on her skin. Neema smiled back, then the two dropped their weapons and inched out of the flora to the gravelly shore.

"Thought that might be you," Evan called out, hopping from a boulder on the other riverbank and shouldering his rifle. "Had to be sure though."

Neema nodded, then scooped some clear water from the river and splashed her face.

"Took you a bit to find us, everything okay?" Evan asked as he crossed the river, hopping on the rocks that protruded from the rapids.

"We're fine. Just wanted to make sure no one followed."

"So what happened to Braden?"

Neema had almost forgotten. Wherever he was, the next time Neema saw him he was in for the ass chewing of his life.

He better be back at camp, she thought. If not, she'd have to figure out another way of dealing with him, but for now all Neema could think of was laying down in her bunk. Even from so far it called to her, and she was sure the others felt the same.

"Got any idea on what we're doin next?" Evan asked while they traversed through the jungle. He asked more questions than anyone Neema had ever known. Sometimes she wished he was more like Jessii and kept quiet.

"Yep," she replied, though she didn't intend on telling him what she was thinking. She still wasn't sure herself, or if any of her ideas would even work. Everything about 'Tem felt like a dream. *You better be as good as I think you are, Milo.*

As they walked into camp a few hours later, Neema checked in with the guards posted at the gate. They hadn't seen Braden pass through. Neema clenched her fists and took deep breaths to hold in her frustration. "Let me know if you see him," she told them.

Neema caught a glimpse of Mezzy speaking with a couple soldiers and unfortunately made eye contact.

"Neema!" she called out, waving an arm.

"I should go check in," Neema said, turning to her squad. "You all go get some rest. It's been a long couple days."

Mezzy finished her conversation and waved Neema inside her tent. "Hang out in here for a minute. I'll be back."

Typical superiors, Neema thought. In such a rush only to make everyone else wait.

Neema paced the tent, which was large as far as tents go. She noted the different amenities Mezzy kept: a small clock, a framed portrait, a collection of tiny, glass figurines, and a dresser large enough that Mezzy couldn't have moved it on her own.

"Before you go snooping through my underwear drawer," Mezzy said, startling Neema, "how bout you tell me what all happened these past few days."

Neema clicked her tongue. "Don't worry, you calling it an 'underwear drawer' tells me everything I need to know." She leaned against the dresser and folded her arms. "You might wanna take a seat."

Neema filled Mezzy in on the evolved yurdrak, the mindless attack, and her rescue mission, but made sure to leave out a few key details like waking up in a magical cave, Braden deserting, and reuniting with Tem.

"The same yurdrak from five years ago?" Mezzy asked.

Neema nodded.

"But it's evolved? We've never heard of a yurdrak evolving before. Are you certain another yurdrak didn't just kill it and eat the insides?"

"I know what I saw, Mez. Milo confirmed it too."

"Milo?"

Neema picked up one of the glass figurines, rolling it between her fingers. "He used to study them or something."

Mezzy laughed, snatching the figurine back and placing it back on the dresser. "Milo was a botanist before he joined the rebellion. Not sure how much drak *studying* he'd've been able to do." She stepped back and opened her arms. "But hey, your squad, right?"

"This is my team for a reason, Mez, I trust them."

"Oh yeah? And what about your other soldier? Check-in claims that you're down a man."

Neema cursed under her tongue that she should've paid those damn guards to keep their mouths shut. "It's nothing, just-"

"Nothing? You have a soldier missing in action, possibly deserted. Also, and this is just a guess, a very educated and thought out guess, you weren't going to tell me about *that* were you?"

"It didn't seem as important as the yurdrak evolution or the mindless army."

Mezzy shifted her weight and crossed her arms in front of her chest. "*I'll* decide what's important. Look, Neema. You can be a great leader…"

"But?"

"You're reckless, and you can only see what's in front of you. Look at the big picture. Then maybe you'll get somewhere."

Where, Mez? In a tent with a figurine collection and an underwear drawer? Neema kept her thoughts to herself but nodded to satiate Mezzy. If she argued, Mezzy would put her on latrine duty.

"You're probably hungry," Mezzy said, motioning to the tent flap she used as a door. "Get some food and rest. We'll talk later."

Neema nodded and left, though there was something she craved more than food. Sweat and dirt clung to her like they were accessories for her outfit, and the baths were a short walk from Mezzy's tent.

Bathe, eat, then sleep. In that order!

Maybe the bath would clear her head some. She walked inside and met a face full of steam. *The fire stones must be extra hot!* Neema looked around, noting the emptiness and still water in each pool. *Must be my lucky day,* she thought. Usually the baths were packed and the water lukewarm. She placed her things on the edge of a pool in the corner, then turned at the sound of splashing water to her right.

Jessii emerged from the pool like a fish fighting a strong current, wheezing ragged breaths.

"Woah! You okay?" Neema asked.

Jessii spun, her eyes wide, teeth clenched, and chest heaving. In the dim torchlight, Neema watched Jessii's cheeks redden. She nodded sheepishly, trying to regain her composure without looking at Neema.

Neema waved, luring Jessii's eyes back to hers. "It's cool, Jessii." Neema hopped over the edge of the pool and sunk in, inch by inch into the stinging heat. Jessii shied away again, this time turning to expose the scars drawn on her back. They reminded Neema of the time she got carried away with a marker as a child.

The two women eased into the pool, calming the sloshing water. "You must've been under a while," Neema said, scrubbing the dirt from her arms and sides. "Surprised the hell outta me!"

Jessii tilted her head to the side and shrugged her shoulders, as if to say that it wasn't a big deal.

Neema chuckled. "Back in the jungle too. That was impressive. You've got some skills."

This time the corner of Jessii's lip turned up, forming what almost looked like a smile.

"Those scars on your back," Neema started, "I've never seen them before. What are they from?"

Jessii's faint smile disappeared, but she nodded to the sword next to the bathtub.

"What happened?"

Jessii shook her head and turned to the side, and Neema picked up on the hint.

"That's okay. I've got my own scars too." Neema lifted out of the water and showed Jessii a long scar above the side of her hip. "See?"

Jessii looked at Neema like she was asking what her scars were from.

"Nope. You don't talk I don't talk."

Jessii grinned, then disappeared underneath the water. She came back up a moment later, running her hands through her hair.

She may be quiet, but at least she's loyal. Unlike Braden... It was like the two were complete opposites.

Neema leaned back and basked in the steam. She hadn't realized how exhausted she was. The pool's heat enveloped her, lulling her muscles into a blissful trance. "Mmm." Neema closed her eyes, ignoring the sound of Jessii leaving her pool.

She felt like she had only closed her eyes for a second when a haunting wind blustered through the baths, jolting Neema awake. What used to be steam was now a thick fog, and Neema's breath added to it.

"Jessii?" she called.

Silence.

She tried to move but couldn't. In front of her, a shadow blacker than a moonless night reached from the corner of the room with tendril-like fingers. At its center was a pair of piercing blue eyes. Neema's body tensed, but she couldn't tear herself from looking at it. The shadow spread, reaching over the lip of her pool, and the unblinking eyes grew closer. It wasn't until the shadow dipped into the water that it began to take shape.

Is it... a person?

A tremendous gust of wind blew her to the side, creating a raging bout of wind and water. Neema had to huddle in the corner to shield herself from the spitting storm.

What is happening!?

As quickly as it began, the squall vanished. Drenched and shivering, Neema turned to where the shadow had been.

"Oh!" she gasped. "Tem!"

He stood at the foot of the pool, his eyes violent tempests.

"Tem," Neema said, covering herself in the pool. "We're going to get you help, so that you can remember, so that you can fight it!"

There was something different about him, even from when she saw him before. He looked... *cold.* From his expression to the paleness of his fingertips. "I don't want to fight it," he finally said.

"Please, Tem! I can help you!" She reached out to him.

He looked down at his hands, and Neema did as well. One held water, the other wind.

"You can't help me." Before Neema could respond, he clapped his hands together, and it was as if he created a blizzard. The temperature dropped, frost covered the walls, and ice spread from his hands to the rest of his body.

He took a single finger and dipped it into the water. The water froze as fast as the ripple spread. Neema still couldn't get out.

"Tem, no! What are you doing?"

The ice crept against her, so cold that it burned. She tried to wriggle free, but the ice inched its way over her body and up her neck, encasing her as if she were an ice cube. Tem was still there, watching her as the ice covered her completely.

Neema's eyes shot open, and she rocked forward. Steaming water splashed over the pool's edge, and Neema desperately filled her lungs, looking around the room. There was no fog, no ice, no shadow. No Tem.

Jessii turned at the sudden noise. She was outside of her pool with a towel, drying herself.

Neema waved to her, as if to say, "It's nothing." *It was just a nightmare,* she thought. Even though the pool was still scorching hot, goosebumps prickled all over her arms. Neema's heart pounded, and she decided she needed to get the hell out of the baths.

What was that? It was so vivid. Neema jumped out of the pool, dried herself off, and threw on some clean clothes, leaving Jessii by herself.

Just a dream, she kept telling herself. But why did she feel so cold?

Chapter Seven

She made a few stops on her way back to the barracks to distract herself. Her dirty clothes needed washed, so she dropped them off at the laundry station, telling the person in charge she was recently promoted to an officer's rank. Then she stopped at the mess tent to fill her empty belly. It wasn't the market in Essence City, but the rebellion cook could whip up a mean serving of fried drak ears.

"Atabo!" she called out, waving down the cook. "Gimme that hot sauce. The special stuff you make." Anything to warm her up from that chilling nightmare.

"You sure, hon?" he asked. "I use hala peppers, straight from this special little spot in the jungle. Spicy!"

"Just give it to me."

"You got it, babe," Atabo said, not noticing her scowl when he called her babe.

She sat in a corner that overlooked the entrance and dug in. The fried drak ears were a little chewy, but still hit the spot. Her lips and mouth felt like she'd kissed a demon straight from the pits of hell. Downing a glass of water only made it worse, and she began to sweat and seethe.

"Oooh!" She sucked in air between her teeth and tried fanning her mouth, but the blazing continued. "Wow! That's good. Really good!" Drawing no attention to herself, she shoveled the rest of her plate in her mouth. Most of the other people in the mess tent were too busy with their own loud conversations to pay her any mind as she left, heading back to the barracks. It had been a few days since she'd been there.

Oh, I miss my bed so much, she thought, feeling the weariness that seeped from her muscles deep within her bones.

It had been a few days since Neema'd been to the dorm, but it was just as she left it. The fried drak ears helped clear her head, so she wasn't as unsettled as before.

I haven't dreamt about Tem in years, she thought, easing into her bunk. They began the night after he was recruited to the army. Memories and pictures formed in her mind. She used to dream Tem was the young watermind that saved them from the burning building during the first yurdrak attack. At the end of the dream, Tem took off after the yurdrak on his own, and the beast was too much for him. She had woken up crying and shivering and alone. It wasn't until she found the rebellion that the dreams stopped.

"Something on your mind?" Evan asked. Neema looked over and found him a few bunks over watching her. A twist of hair dangled in front of his eye as he hunched over the top bunk. He was shirtless and clean shaven. Neema took notice of the smooth curves of skin that wrapped tight against his abdominal muscles.

Does he shave all over? Neema wondered for a moment. Now all she could think of was shaving her legs. She hadn't done it since she prepared for her mission back in Essence City. *I don't know if I'll ever take a bath again after that damn dream though.*

"Nah, just thinking about a few things," she replied, crossing one leg over the other. She began running her fingers up and down the bits of soft hair on her calf.

"Thanks for coming back for us, Neema. You're a good leader."

Neema nodded the comment away, "Mm. No prob."

Evan hopped down off his bunk and scratched the back of his head, shadows diving into the recesses of muscle on his body. "Hey, umm... I know how it gets out here. If you ever want someone to hang out with, as an escape or anything. I could-"

Neema snorted. "Don't get me wrong, you're very pretty, Evan, and with a body like that I'm sure you'd be *great* in bed." Neema collapsed on her back and reached her hands underneath her pillow. "But I don't screw my subordinates."

"Right," Evan said. "Sorry, ma'am."

"Sorry? Don't apologize, Ev. Though you should probably get whatever you need out of your system. I don't want you jacking off in my barracks."

"Did I come at a bad time?" Milo asked, the door shutting softly behind him.

Neema snickered. "No, but Ev's about to. Aren't ya? Hey, I think Milo could give you a hand."

Milo slapped Evan's butt on the way to his bunk. "You're not quite my type, E. I like a guy with a little more meat on his bones. I'd break you in half, boy."

"I think it's safe to say the mood has passed. Thank you all for that." Evan climbed back up on his bunk.

"Anytime, Ev." Neema said. "Just remember, if I see that blanket moving vigorously tonight I'm gonna send Milo up there."

Milo blew Evan a kiss and sat down, pulling books and notepads from his bag.

"I found my research on what we were talking about before, Neema," Milo said. "There's enough here for me to get some plans started."

Sleep felt like it was such a welcome thing before, but now Neema was too stimulated to think about it. She nodded to Milo, "Okay, but first… I hear you were into botany before all this. What's up with that?"

Milo nodded, and his eyes drifted toward the floor. "Yeah, I was a botanist before the rebellion. That's what I *did*. Not who I was." He held up a weathered leather-bound journal, stuffed full of notes and labels. "*This* is me."

Neema chewed on his response. "This is everything to me, Milo."

He met her eyes and held her gaze for a few precious seconds. "I know it is, Neema."

"Good."

While Milo sifted through his notes, she took the extra time to tinker with her elemental rods, replacing the lightning stone she had taken out. She didn't have a spare fire stone though, so she made a mental note to keep an eye out for one.

"Here," Milo said, handing her a sheet of paper. It was filled with sketches for the device, which essentially looked like a collar.

I need some supplies for this, she thought. "I'm heading over to the depot. Anyone need any requisitions?"

Milo was nose deep in his research, and Evan only grunted, so she hopped up from the bed and grabbed her jacket, swinging it around her shoulders.

"Keep an eye on Ev, Milo. No beating off!"

Once she stepped outside, the cool night air nipped through the opening in her jacket and right through her tank-top. She pulled the jacket together and buttoned it up, then shoved her hands inside the pockets. Throughout the day it was hot, sunny, and beautiful up here, but at night a chill crept in from the sea.

The camp was still full of movement. Neema passed by a squad returning from patrol. Their shoulders were slumped and faces drained. Neema knew the feeling. The few weeks they've been on patrol had been taxing. She nodded to the woman at the front of the group and smiled. The woman nodded in return and passed by. A breeze filled with scents from the jungle drifted along with them.

"What we do is important," Neema told herself out loud. "Patrol most of all." Without patrol squadrons, the camp might get overrun by a sudden mindless attack or draks or worse. *Still doesn't mean I have to like it, and I'd rather be out taking down the king and his cronies.* She kept that thought to herself. *Patience, Neema.*

She nodded to the requisition officer. He was an older man with a graying beard and a gimp leg. "Officer" was a loose term. He wore a baggy pair of pants, a loose tunic, muttered to himself, and had a shaking leg. He stuck out the sign-in form with jittery hands, and Neema plucked it up and signed in.

"Just need some spare metal. Say… have ya got any extra fire stones, Jib?" she asked the man.

"Nah," Jib grumbled.

"Even for me?" Neema leaned over and batted her eyelashes.

Jib turned and started muttering to himself again. Neema fished a coin from her pocket, then reached down the front of her shirt like she pulled it from her bra. "How bout now?"

Jib looked at the coin, then to Neema's chest. He snatched it up with a filthy hand and inspected it, which included biting and sniffing it.

Pervert, she thought, holding down the urge to hurl.

Jib winked and nodded over to the requisition tent. "Fire shtone in there fer ya, shweetie."

Neema smiled and walked away, feeling Jib's eyes on her backside as she slipped inside of the tent. "Gross," she muttered under her breath. *The rebellion attracts all kinds.*

A few lanterns glowed in the tent, casting shadows along the supply crates. Rifles lined the wall, along with other bits of gear and supplies. She'd been in here before, so she knew that the elemental stones were in a crate in the corner.

The fire stone was right on top, casting an orange light on the rest of the crate. Neema peeked in the lower level, finding a water stone and a wind stone. She thought about taking them too, but Jib would know and find her if he needed them. There were a dozen or so power chips scattered in the crate, so she scooped those up and pocketed them. *He won't miss em.*

"You got a requisition order for that fire stone? Those things aren't easy to get ya know."

The flap to the tent swung shut behind Mezzy. Neema closed the crate and turned. "Ever heard of knocking?"

Mezzy laughed. "It's a damn tent, Neema, where am I supposed to knock?" She nodded. "You gonna tell me what you're doin?"

Neema shook her head. "Nope."

"Let me guess. It's for the good of the rebellion? Don't tell me you made a deal with Jib. He's *disgusting*."

"Whattaya want, Mez?"

"Not in the talking mood, huh? Well, I got a report that a blonde male

was running around toward the Deadlands. Probably Braden. Here."
Mezzy handed the report over, and Neema skimmed through it. A patrol
saw him from a distance while returning from a route but didn't pursue.
Neema met Mezzy's eyes, then looked back to the file.

"I'll take care of it."

"Good! Do this right, and your patrol days may near their end."

"I won't be going," Neema corrected. "I'll send someone from my
squad."

"Delegating, huh?" Mezzy raised an eyebrow. "That doesn't sound
like you."

"You ever do anything with that yurdrak intel I gave you?"

Mezzy tilted her head to the side. "Always on alert."

Neema gave her a look, nodded, and left the tent. Jib had the rest of
her requisition ready, which he handed to her. His hand tried to graze hers
as she grabbed the pack, but she yanked it away too fast.

"Bye, Shweetheart," he said. "Shee you soon."

"Kiss my ass, Jib." Neema saluted with the fire stone and trotted
away. Again, she felt his eyes on her, and she wished her jacket was long
enough to cover her butt. She eyed the baths again, weighing whether she
should take another before deciding against it.

The barracks were quiet aside from Evan's snoring, and Milo was
nose deep in his research, though his eyes drooped heavily. Jessii sat up
on her bunk, and it looked like she wasn't doing anything at all except
sitting there.

"Jessii," Neema whispered. Her hair was silhouetted against the
moonlit window, and the side of her head that was shaved glowed faintly.

Jessii hopped off the bunk, landing with a huff. She nodded to Neema
as if to ask what she needed, then ran her hair back behind her ear.

"I have a mission for you."

Jessii's lips twitched.

"Braden is making a mess out by the Deadlands. He needs to be brought in for questioning on desertion. I'd like you to do it. On your own."

"You're sending Jessii on a *solo* target mission?" Evan asked. Apparently he wasn't sleeping.

Neema ignored Evan, looking at Jessii for an acknowledgment. Jessii nodded and grabbed her bag. Neema smiled.

No nonsense, she thought. Something in Jessii's eyes told Neema that she had experience and confidence to succeed in her task.

She handed Jessii the file. The quiet woman flipped through it quickly, then made eye contact with Neema and nodded. She started to walk off, but Neema put a hand on Jessii's shoulder.

Neema whispered, "Now don't go getting any new scars. I want you back safe, okay?"

Jessii's lip twisted slightly into a smile, and she nodded with a quick shift of her neck. Evan hopped off of his bunk to speak with Jessii further, so Neema gave them their privacy as she slid into her bunk, wishing for warmer dreams of Tem.

*****

Sizaal watched from the branches of one of the largest trees in the forest. With his eyes, he could see across the entire jungle, searching for the human girl he saved.

A nearby bird hovered, then settled on his shoulder. It peered down to the ground, searching for a grub or worm to eat. Her nest was in the next tree over with three baby chicks inside, squawking for food.

There was something special about this Neema. "Could she be my ally?" he asked himself. *"Perhaps I'll show her the true way of the elements."*

Sizaal created a handful of seeds, giving them to the bird. It flew off, joyful to bring dinner to its young. He jumped from the tree and landed, using his earth heart to lessen the thud and meld with the ground.

"I must see the guardstone. It will know what to do."

He took one last look toward the shore and nodded.

"Be safe, Neema. I feel dangerous movement in the winds. Pra'tear weaves a treacherous web, and I fear it will be the end of us all."

Chapter Eight

Jessii walked into the night and through camp, catching sight of Neema's superior, Mezzy, while walking to the beach. Jessii warmed at the mere sound of her strong, penetrating voice. *She's not like me*, Jessii thought, giving the woman a wide berth to avoid any unnecessary embarrassment.

The crescent moon hung high in the sky, and the surrounding stars twinkled. Any clouds up there didn't obstruct her view, and the night was a kind shade of blue, perfect for traveling.

I'll follow the beach for a little while, then break off into the jungle to camp, she told herself. The soothing waves calmed her, and the elements were rich here.

Evan's words echoed in her mind. "Be careful," he said a hundred times. They may have been twins, but he didn't know enough about her to worry so much.

I can take care of myself, she thought, *and now is my chance to prove it.*

Jessii hopped down a series of boulders and landed in the sand, the noise barely a whisper amongst the waves massaging the shore. She smiled. *Quiet and quick.*

As she tracked through the sand, her thoughts transitioned to Neema. *She's different from Evan. I was wrong about her.* She didn't notice it until earlier today. The world worked mysteriously, but she and Neema were brought together for a reason. Not for love. No, Neema was haunted by something in her past. A boy, for certain.

Would the world put so much faith in us? Jessii picked up a random rock, then ran up and jumped with a spin, throwing the rock at a made up target in her head. *Bullseye!*

Surely the world had better options to choose from, but then again, maybe there weren't. Maybe things were that bad.

Something awful will happen.

Soon, Jessii strayed from the beach and its calming waters, treading into the forest. Night had the island completely covered, so it was time to find a suitable spot to camp for the night.

I'll sleep for a couple hours, then get back to finding Braden.

In the forest, Jessii stayed in the darkness. Bits of moonlight stabbed through the gaps in the canopy, striking the forest floor. Jessii avoided those areas. Better to not be seen or heard in the forest at this time of night. Draks weren't the only predators to be mindful of. She did her best, but Jessii knew there were eyes out there, watching her.

Try it, Jessii whispered in her mind, while keeping one hand on the hilt of her katana, Sorya.

Up ahead, a shadow danced across a splinter of moonlight, and Jessii stopped cold. She closed her eyes, they were useless in this dark anyway, and listened. The silent void swallowed her, and inside it bugs buzzed from tree to tree, a breeze caressed two leaves in an embrace, and a churoki up above strained on a branch, peering down at her. Jessii tilted her head, *There's something else.* It waited in front of her, causing the rest of the forest to still. Then she heard its throaty growl and the glow of green, cat-like eyes.

I'm not so easy a kill, she tried to communicate to the creature.

Up ahead it sniffed, filling its nostrils with her scent and bloodlust. It wouldn't listen to her warning. The beast's mind was already made up. It yearned for blood, meat, and flesh. Jungle cats got that way when they were desperate.

The earth will thank me for your sacrifice.

Jessii lunged, and the cat pounced. Suddenly the forest came to life, jeering monkeys cheered like a crowd in a gladiator duel, calling for death. Smaller animals scurried away, hoping to not get in the middle of the fight. Jessii kept her eyes closed and unleashed her sword. She sliced through air, and the cat ducked underneath. Jessii fell and rolled to the side before the panther could dig into her with its claws. Its paws thudded on the ground and it moved with a quickness that surprised Jessii given the beast's size. Judging from the sound, it was bigger than any jungle cat she'd ever encountered. Already, it was upon her, striking her leg before she could swing again.

"Rgghhh!" she growled and spun away, punching the panther with the hilt of her sword. The warm blood that trickled from her leg drew the panther into more of a frenzy, but she fended it off again with a wide sweep.

Jessii stopped her spin with a skidding halt and placed a hand on the ground. She breathed deep. *I have to end this.* The panther snarled and pounced again, but this time Jessii jumped off her good leg high into the air. She twirled like a dancer, knowing the panther was just beneath her, then plunged the sword deep within the panther's neck. The panther's scream cut off as they tumbled back to the ground, blood spilling from the beast onto Jessii's clothes and hair, pooling on the jungle floor. The raucous crowd around her silenced.

None of them expected her to come out the victor. None but the earth below, grateful for the sacrifice.

Jessii sighed and clambered to her feet. Every limb shook with adrenaline, but pain from the exertion and the wound on her leg started to spread. She stalked off, leaving the carcass and the commotion. She'd need to do something about the cut on her leg. If she remembered right, there should be a stream not far.

I can clean it and make camp there, she thought.

"Ah!" she winced, pushing off too much on her injured leg. In her pack, she had some cloth, so she wrapped her leg as well as she could. It would have to do until she made it to the stream.

Jessii limped her way for almost an hour before she found it, hissing with each breath by that time. She carefully removed her makeshift bandage and pants, causing the wound to bleed more.

I have to if I don't want to risk infection, she thought, cringing at the icy touch of the stream. The ointment that followed burned so much she screamed, and her eyes welled with tears.

This'll need stitches, Jessii knew. It would make traveling difficult, but as long as she didn't get into another fight with a jungle cat she'd be okay. Once stitched, cleaned, and bandaged, Jessii could barely keep her eyes open.

She weighed her options. *Build a fire? Or climb up and sleep in the tree?* Her body yearned for the warmth of the fire, especially after that dip in the freezing stream. It was smarter to sleep in the tree though.

If a mindless patrol comes by, I'll be dead before I wake up. I'll set up a quick noisemaker to alert me if another cat wants to cross me.

Jessii climbed up a nearby tree that appeared suitable, her muscles straining as she tried not to use her leg. She made it about twenty feet up and found a good collection of branches she could curl up on. The night sky peaked through, dark indigo salted with glimmering stars. Jessii pulled a shawl around her and stared up for a while, but it wasn't long before she drifted to sleep.

By Antonio Baldari

*****

"Hey, Mezzy!" Neema called out. Her superior turned, her blazing, red hair shining in the morning sunlight.

Mezzy saw Neema and instantly looked the other way. Neema couldn't tell if she was cursing, spitting, or deciding whether to run away. Whatever it was made Neema smile.

Mezzy let out a deep breath and nodded to Neema as her, Evan, and Milo approached. "So you sent Jessii to retrieve Braden. Gotta say, your group looks a lot better when she's around. Why are you packed for patrol? I gave you the day off."

"We switched with Jacko's squad," Neema said. "Figured those lazy jerks could use the day off more than us."

Mezzy narrowed her eyes at each of them before speaking. "But that means you'll be on patrol for four days straight."

Neema smiled and nodded back at Milo and Evan, "Hence, that's why we've got all this gear."

Mezzy stepped up close enough so Neema could make out Mezzy's eyelashes curling out from her hazel eyes. "You've been a pain in my ass since we got back from the city. Dodging patrols, complaining about every little duty, and now here you are going above and beyond, and you know what?" She waited for an answer.

Neema raised an eyebrow in response.

"As much as I'm telling myself that this is a bad idea... go ahead." She looked south, toward Essence City. "There's something happening out there, and if you're on top of it we might just have a chance against it."

Neema curled her lip up into a smile, and Mezzy raised a finger.

"That's *not* free rein to do whatever the hell you want. Go patrol and

111

come back. Just don't bring that monster or any mindless back with you."

Mezzy slapped Neema's rear and stomped off, shouting orders and pointing at other soldiers.

That went better than I thought. Neema turned back and nodded to Milo and Evan. Milo smirked, and Evan looked unusually apprehensive.

"Come on, Ev!" she hung onto his shoulder as they left camp. "Jessii is just fine, and what we're doing isn't so bad. I need you to *trust* me."

Evan slowly nodded. "You got it, boss lady. I hope you're right about this."

Me too.

*****

"I've seen this," the guardstone, Arlac, said within Sizaal's mind. It looked through Sizaal's memories of Neema and her actions. "The woman could be an ally."

"She is stubborn, I can sense it already." Sizaal said. "What if she is unwilling?"

"You must persuade her, by whatever means you can." The voice pulsed in Sizaal's mind, powerful but soothing. "Bring her here, and I will show her the truth, but be aware of Pra'tear. He has been trying to find me and release his true form. If he obtains my power he will bend the world to his will. Reality itself could be altered."

"I understand," Sizaal said, rising to pursue his task.

"There's one more thing," the guardstone said. "You know what has happened to the beast?"

"Yes. It is now a yurdrakon. I will stay clear of its path."

"That's not all. Earth and fire sing with harmony inside of the beast. The two elements have created a life stone, a most powerful item. If

Pra'tear obtains it, he can use it to change form without my remaining power."

"Why hasn't he destroyed it already? He has the ability."

"We are players in a dangerous game, Sizaal. Pra'tear doesn't know what creates the life stone. Just that it is brought forward from the monster. If it gets close to the city, he will sense its presence and act on it. Until then, he will let the creature wreak havoc on the humans purely for his twisted pleasure."

Sizaal nodded. "There is a balance of knowledge and power. I will retrieve the girl." He turned to go, but Arlac's presence halted him.

"One more thing before you go, sanctor."

"Yes?"

"There is something in the temple you must retrieve for me. I've embedded the memory within you, and it will activate as you enter the ruins. Go there first, and make haste!"

Sizaal engaged his earth heart and travelled within the ground to return to the surface. He'd used his wind heart too often recently, so he let it rejuvenate with the passing winds around him. Instead of flying, he merged back with the ground and earth travelled. It wasn't as fast, but it would save him time.

Time was of the essence.

*****

Jessii woke at the first sliver of sunlight, which meant she slept over an hour longer than she hoped. And she was that much further behind Braden.

I'm already at a disadvantage because of my stupid leg. Jessii frowned. Her leg was sore and stiff, but in the light she could see that she did a good job with the bandaging.

I'll need to change it before I set off, she thought. It would set her back, but it was the smart thing to do. Jessii climbed down the tree, her body cramped, cold, and sore, groaning at the early morning strain.

As Jessii reached the forest floor, a slight breeze wafted a lemony scent her way. *Lillyfalls? That will help.* Jessii looked throughout the forest and found the flowers a dozen or so meters away, the bright, yellow blooms catching her eye. In the dead of night they would have retreated, and she'd never have known they were there. Some plants were funny like that. She plucked a handful and stuffed them in her pack, then grabbed a few more and returned to the stream.

Hmm. Jessii looked around. *There. That will work.* She grabbed a couple suitable rocks and ground the flowers into a pulp, then took off her bandage and applied it to her cut. Already, soothing sensations rippled from her legs to the rest of her body.

"Ah," Jessii sighed aloud. *Time to go.*

Finding Braden's trail wasn't hard. She found the approximate location where Braden was sighted fleeing the patrol squad, and immediately found an identifiable path of broken twigs, footprints, and other signs of travel.

As she picked up the pace, her muscles started to warm and loosen. She nibbled on a lillyfall. The soothing flower did wonders for her mind, not just her body, easing her foul mood along with her cramping.

The forest began to open up into clearings. The rich foliage and strong trees gave way to dry, cracking earth. *I'm getting closer,* Jessii thought. The Deadlands were an hour or so south, but judging from Braden's tracks he wasn't far. He made camp multiple times since fleeing patrol. *I need to catch him fast. Can't let him get too far into the Deadlands.* It would be much harder to track him.

Why would he go there? Jessii asked herself. No one went there unless they wanted to die. *Braden's too weak for death,* she thought.

She slowed as she deciphered the trail ahead. The clearing let out right into the hot sands of the Deadlands; a scorching, windy abyss. There was something about the trail though. It led right to the Deadlands, as if…

It's deliberate.

Just then a branch snapped to her side. *I've walked right into a trap!*

Logs thudded to the ground all around her, and ropes whipped from the surrounding trees. Jessii pushed off to make a run for it, but her leg was still in pain and wasn't fast enough. The net caught her and drove her skyward, and she bounced, the thick ropes digging into her.

"Kst!" Jessii cursed, reaching for her sword. More logs clumped to the ground, and another set of ropes dropped from above and held her in place. She couldn't move.

"Well, well, well!" a voice sounded from below. Jessii looked sideways down at Braden emerging from a dead, hollowed out tree. He put his hands on his hips and looked sideways back at her. "Jess?"

Of course it's me, you moron. Now cut me down!

Braden walked closer, so that he was directly underneath her. "I gotta admit, dearie, I figured it would be Neema that'd be sent after me. You just won't do."

Wait, what? Neema?

"I'm sorry it has to be this way, but I can't let you out of there alive. You see, if I leave you up there, you'll eventually wiggle that sword from its scabbard and cut yourself free. It's true, you don't say much, but I know you, Jess. You'll keep coming after me. And where I'm going you don't want any part. I'm doing you a favor, really!"

Aw crap. Jessii wriggled her hand furiously to try to get to her sword.

Braden slid a knife smoothly from inside his jacket sleeve and spun it in his hand.

"Sorry, dearie."

He sliced through the rope just as Jessii's fingers wrapped around Sorya's hilt. The ground rushed forward as she plummeted, and all she could do was tuck herself into a ball.

Hold tight!

She crashed into the ground with a thud, unforgiving, and it knocked the air from her lungs. Jessii collapsed and rolled along the ground, stars popping up in her eyes.

Don't pass out, don't pass out, don't pass out!

Jessii gasped for air as Braden's shadow loomed over her. His knife was still in his hand, and in an instant he struck. Jessii rolled, swinging Sorya with the scabbard still on. The sword and knife collided with a loud thwack.

Braden looked taken aback for a second before he dashed to the side, then lunged again. It was too late. Jessii had her blade and half of the net off her. She already was on the offensive.

You picked the wrong moon phase to screw with me, Braden.

Metal rang loudly against metal as their blades clashed. Braden brought out his other knife to outmaneuver her with two weapons. Jessii's side ached, the bandage on her leg was red with blood, and her vision was still fuzzy from the fall, but she let instinct flow through her. *Block right, parry left, duck and slide, then spin and strike.* She danced, kicked up dirt, and swung through the air. Braden deflected and dodged her at each step, but he wasn't at her level. She was born, bred, and trained for this. He merely lacked the will to keep up with her.

Braden smiled as he closed in, where his shorter knives would give him the advantage. What he didn't realize was that her blade was already at his leg, slicing through cloth, skin, and muscle. He winced and stepped back, but Jessii spun, kicking him square in his pretty jaw. One more smack with the butt of her sword and he fell, unconscious.

Jessii spat blood from her lip, then immediately went to work, binding Braden's hands and legs with rope from his trap. She gave him enough slack in his legs so he could walk, but it would be very taxing for him. Then she tied him to a tree while she meticulously searched her body for every scrape, bruise, and cut that needed bandaged.

Once done, she needed to tend to Braden's wounds. The only wound needing attention was the cut she inflicted on his leg. It wouldn't do if he were to get an infection and die before they made it back to camp. Perhaps that was for the best. Why would he lay a trap like this anyway if he was deserting? What was really going on?

Jessii squirted some ointment on Braden's cut, and the man jolted awake.

"Ah!" he cried out. "What the?" He took a look at his surroundings and cursed. "So what am I now, your prisoner? Shit…"

Jessii rubbed the salve in, covering the entire cut.

"Watch it, will ya!? Fuck, that burns!"

Jessii smacked on a gob of the lillyfall pulp, then wrapped his bandage tight.

"Ooh, that feels good," he moaned, leaning back. "Yeah, get that nice and tight. You know, love, you could take care of some other business while you're down there." Braden smiled devilishly.

Just because I don't talk doesn't mean I can't hear you, jackass.

Jessii pressed on his bandaged thigh slightly, enough to make him squirm in pain. Then she cocked her head to the side and raised her eyebrows, as if to ask him if he wanted to keep talking.

"Nope, nope. I got it! You're not into that. I get it. No worries, dearie. Please let go!"

Jessii smirked and started undoing the knot that kept him tied against the tree.

"So you think these bonds are going to hold me, huh?" Braden scoffed. "We'll see about that."

Try me.

Jessii let the rope fall to the ground, and like a wild dog Braden took off. He made it two steps before he fell flat, coughing up dirt.

"Aghhhh!" he kicked his legs in protest, the ropes binding his legs so that he could only kick them as far as a small child.

Well that's a fitting picture. Jessii grabbed the line of rope and tugged, pulling Braden along as she walked.

"No, see, I don't want to go *that* way," he said. "I want to go *this* way." He nodded toward the Deadlands.

Jessii shook her head and tugged on his leash. In return, Braden planted his feet and refused to move.

"I don't think you heard me," he said. "I'm not going that way, sweetheart."

Braden was much larger than she was. She'd never be able to pull him along if he wouldn't walk.

I could always knock him out and build a cart to roll him along in, Jessii thought. *No, I suppose there are other options.*

Jessii dug into Braden's pack, fishing out some snacks. He looked around and finally noticed all he had on him were the clothes on his back.

"You devilish cunt," he sneered.

Jessii raised an eye at that. *What happened to all that charm, Braden?*

He looked as if he didn't care, but she opened the package and popped one of the crispy biscuits into her mouth. Then she crunched down, making sure he heard every little bite. *Mmm, salty*, she thought. *This should get my point across.*

While she ate, Jessii rummaged through the rest of his things. The slight jingle of coin caught her attention, so she grabbed the bag and shook it around for him to see. With a smile she dropped the coins into her own pack.

"Really?" he questioned. "Now that's uncalled for."

As she kept going through his pack, she took out his knives to better see inside. At the sight of them, Braden tensed just enough for her to notice.

Gotcha.

Jessii dropped the pack and moved to throw the knives out into the waves of sand in the Deadlands. With today's winds they wouldn't last long before disappearing like a seashell caught by the tide.

"Okay, wait!" he yelled, raising his arms as far as his bindings would let him. "You win! You win! Just, don't get rid of those. They're important to me."

Jessii stared at him, measuring his authenticity. *That will do.* She tossed the knives back into his pack, then tossed a crisped biscuit his way. He caught it with his mouth in midair and crunched down.

"Mmm," he sighed. "So good."

Now that I've got you trained, little puppy, let's play follow the leader. Jessii nodded in the direction back toward camp and tugged on Braden's leash. He followed, and their slow jaunt back to camp began.

Braden couldn't learn quick enough that she was in charge,

complaining and stalling every way he could.

"My bonds are too tight," he whined. Jessii yanked him on, contemplating whether she should tighten them further.

"I have to take a leak," he groaned. She stopped and let him, but stood at his back in case he tried anything funny.

"But I'm hungry," he moaned. Every mile or so she'd pop back crispy biscuits. One for her, and one for him. She normally didn't like foods as salty as this, but she made an exception. Braden didn't catch every one, so at times he'd have to drop to the ground to pick it up with his mouth. He'd eat it, dirt and all.

Jessii's leg and side rippled with pain at each step and every time she had to pull on Braden's leash. It was getting harder and harder to mask the pain, so she stopped at the sound of water up ahead. Looking around, she found a tree large enough for a guy as tall as Braden. She corralled him against it and loosened some of his bonds.

"Finally," he sighed. Jessii lifted his arms by the rope and tied him to a thick, low-hanging branch of the tree. "Wait, what are you- are you serious!? My arms are going to fall straight off my damn body. This is ridiculous. Help! HELP!"

Jessii finished binding him firmly enough so he wouldn't weasel out of it, then slapped him hard across the face with an open palm. Bits of saliva and blood flew from his mouth, but he shut up.

"I'm going to make you pay for all this, Jess," Braden said. "Then you'll see who I *really* am."

Jessii stared into his eyes, they were unyielding and deep.

How many masks do you wear, Braden? Jessii asked. She wasn't sure if she ever wanted to find out what was beneath them.

After visually double checking his bonds, she trotted off, out of sight and toward the river. It was time to care for herself while he was secure. She stripped down and cleaned all of her wounds in the cold, shallow water. The cut on her leg was healing nicely, but not as fast as she wanted. Her side was bruised purple from her breast to her hip, but she could deal with the pain so long as she didn't hit it on anything.

Jessii quickly dried, applied new bandages, and put her clothes back on.

Maybe we'll camp here for the night, she thought, heading back toward where she left Braden. *We can wake up before the sun and make it back before lunch.*

Jessii walked through the trees, and a loose breeze prickled her skin, pushing her hair to the side. A few large-beaked gligrows perched on the tree branches, not paying her any mind as dusk settled on the evening. At that moment, a nearby reptile snapped its tongue on a buzzing insect, and Jessii felt something change in the surrounding air.

That's odd, she thought, scanning back and forth through the drooping leaves. She rounded a thick, rotted out tree trunk and turned to where she left Braden. Her heart jumped at the sight, then began pounding with adrenaline. Braden was gone.

She started to turn, but the movement beside her was too fast. Braden landed a crushing kick right on her bad leg, and then slammed his fist into her bruised side. Her body exploded in pain, and tears gushed from her eyes. Jessii tried to get back up and fight, but Braden had the advantage and wasn't giving up.

With one more punch he sent Jessii spinning into the mud, the world fading to black around her.

Chapter Nine

Sizaal ascended the ridge and looked out to the east coast string of beaches. Here, the rocks nearly outnumbered the grains of sand, but it was the home of the old guardstone temple. Waves splashed against the rocks, and birds chirped and fished. This area had been left untouched since Pra'tear seized control of the guardstone's powers.

"But what did you do here, old friend?" Sizaal asked out loud. To the unskilled eye, it appeared as a run down, abandoned temple overlooking the sea. The humans never found it, because Pra'tear would never let his mindless soldiers wander close enough to it.

Sizaal descended the rocky path toward the courtyard. Crystalline statues lined the pathways, most were run down, cracked, and in pieces scattered about the area. The ruins of the temple rose up ahead in the middle of a pool of water.

It used to glimmer gold in the never-ending sunshine, Sizaal remembered. *Now it is covered in dirt and tarnish.*

Sizaal thought of using some of his Essence to bring beauty back to the area, but thought better of it. He'd need that power in the coming battle.

"And I suppose something is lying in wait for me here as well."

Clouds blocked out the sun overhead, keeping any light from reflecting off the pools and streams that intertwined with the pathways making up the courtyard. Sizaal's steps clicked on the smooth stone, and aside from the waves across the beach it was quiet.

The animals don't come near here either. Hmm. What curses this place?

He stepped up the final incline to the temple and used his earth heart to raise the bridge. The ground beneath him grumbled, and the pool's waters subsided to reveal the new pathway. Sizaal attempted to step onto the path, but his leg was suspended in midair, unable to move forward.

Sizaal couldn't speak nor retreat away from the temple. It was as if it held him there. He stood for several minutes, gauging what abilities he could use. All of his elemental hearts were beating, but he couldn't manipulate anything outside of his body.

This is Pra'tear's doing! I should've known he would defile this sacred place.

As he attempted to move physically again, he noticed something. This was a barrier trap.

Hmm. Created using the elements. Now what happens if I...

RELEASE, Sizaal Spoke, the gestures were still embedded in his memory. He stumbled, yet regained his footing.

The Language still has power here, Sizaal thought. What else could it do?

Sizaal walked forward along the pathway, and water swished about beneath him. As he neared the entrance to the temple, his vision went fuzzy. The guardstone's memory appeared in his mind, and Sizaal dropped to one knee.

The memory unfolded before him like he was transported back in time. The cracked stone melded together, the sun began to shine, bathing Sizaal in warmth and the reflecting rays of the nearby pools. Flowers bloomed in every color all around him. A twinkle of light caught his eye, coming from inside the temple.

"Could it be?" Sizaal asked himself.

He continued walking the path through the pool to the temple. Its doors were cracked open so he couldn't quite see, but Sizaal knew the light from within's source. The guardstones.

"We have kept this balance for generations," one of them, Re'la, said. "We must continue to keep it!"

"I fear the time for that may be too late," Arlac said. "An eclipse is coming, and with it another weapon will be born."

"We must obtain it to secure its power," Re'la said.

"Have Pra'tear retrieve it. He is our most experienced sanctor," the center guardstone, Yor, said.

"Hmm," Arlac grumbled. "Is that wise? His temper is questionable, and the eclipse stone can reveal certain truths-"

The memory faded as another began. This time, Sizaal was back in Arlac's cave, standing before the last remaining guardstone.

"Why am I here?" Sizaal asked.

"Sizaal," the guardstone spoke. "The artifact you seek is hidden amongst the ruin. Re'la sealed it to keep it out of Pra'tear's grasp. Another eclipse is coming, and its shadow will have lasting repercussions."

"What is this eclipse stone?" Sizaal asked.

"It is one of the absolute forms of Essence. That, along with my power, may be enough to defeat Pra'tear."

"How can he be that powerful? After everything that's happened?"

"There are other stones that contain absolute Essence. Just one of them is all he needs."

"For what? What is Pra'tear's goal?"

"Make haste, Sanctor. Bring me the eclipse stone and the girl."

The vision dissipated as if it were fog cleared by the late morning sun. Sizaal found himself in the middle of the temple, surrounded by scattered relics. He hadn't been here in decades, back when the guardstones controlled the way of things. Now, being in the temple reminded him of how orderly the world had once been.

But what lies in the future?

A glimmer caught Sizaal's gaze, faint and unremarkable. But how could something twinkle with no light? He moved forward, to where the former altar stood, now a fractured slab of rock. A burning ring surrounded a stone as dark as death.

The eclipse stone, Sizaal thought as he plucked it from the ground, expecting to feel the stone's Essence within. *Nothing,* he thought. *I feel nothing.*

*****

Jessii could've sworn she only blacked out for a few seconds, but she was already bound just as she did to Braden not long before. Her senses were slow in returning, but in a few more seconds all the pain rippled over her. She felt the warm tracks of blood on her leg as a fresh drop rolled down, and her face ached worse than her side. Daunting shadows lurked from every angle, as if they were alive and about to pull her down to whatever depths they emerged from.

Braden must've hit me, Jessii thought.

"You up, dearie?" Braden asked. Jessii couldn't see him, but his voice was off to the side. "I've been waitin. See, you've made things very difficult for me. I just wanted to run off and be left alone, but no, no. You had to go and fuck that up with your stupid sword and leash, toting me around like a damn dog."

Heh, yeah I did. And I will again. Just gotta figure a way out of this. Just gotta-

Braden grabbed her face, squeezing her cheeks.

Jessii winced. *Ouch, dude. That hurts!*

"I'll bet some people say you're pretty, don't they?"

Huh?

"See you're not quite my type. Oh, and so we're clear, I'm going to be killing you."

This again? I thought we were over this. Why does my head hurt so bad?

"Hmm," Braden let his hand fall from her cheek to her neck, never straying from her skin.

Don't touch me.

Braden smiled, but didn't bare any teeth as he did. He narrowed his eyes like a scavenger ready to feast on its meal. Braden leaned in real close, so that his breath fluttered against Jessii's ear. She knew he was smelling her hair.

"Mmm, you just washed up, didn't you? Don't worry, I won't kill you quite yet. I have to make you pay first!" He slid a knife from his sleeve.

Where did you get- All of Jessii's things were gone. Her pack, sword, his pack. All she had were the clothes on her back. *How did this happen?*

Jessii started to take note of Braden's body language, just as he ran the blade across her arm. He did it slow and methodical, deliberate. The tip of

126

the blade bit into her flesh, searing and hot. Jessii clenched her jaw, but otherwise didn't move.

"I've always wondered what you sound like, Jess," Braden said. "I want to hear you. That's all! Then we'll be done."

This time he dragged the tip of the blade from her shoulder down her chest, not digging into skin, more like he was exploring her body with the knife, trying to find out where he should cut next.

"Say my name, sweetheart."

You're sick.

Braden lowered the knife down to Jessii's navel, pausing there for a moment.

"Here's how this'll work, love. I'm going to do terrible, *unspeakable* things to you. The only way I'll stop is if you…

Say.

My.

Name."

Jessii tensed, bracing herself for whatever torture Braden had ready in his thoughts. She tried to mute the world around her and close off all her senses, but there was some distant force she couldn't expel no matter how hard she tried. As it intruded on her thoughts, Braden's knife circled her waist, digging deeper and deeper.

Is that water? The river, maybe? No, I was just there, it didn't rage like this.

Braden's hand wrapped around her hip, but it retreated as the water became a deafening roar.

"Ah, shit," Braden cursed under his breath. "Ho, fellas! Nothin to see here."

Jessii opened her eyes and saw what kept Braden from continuing his torture. Three waterminds stood in front of her. Their clouded eyes shifted as if they regarded Braden and her one at a time.

Help me, Jessii thought.

One of the waterminds tilted their head at her, then looked to Braden and held out a hand. Water bubbled and formed in his palm, "Move away."

"You don't know what's really going on here, chums," Braden said. "The lady and I, we're just-"

The watermind that spoke blasted Braden, and the other two flanked both sides. Water detained Braden against the tree while the others held him firmly.

"This isn't right! You don't know who I am!" Braden shouted.

"Rebel," the watermind said.

"No! No! I'm not with them! I'm with *you*! I swear! *She's* the rebel!" Braden jabbed a finger at Jessii, but the two mindless soldiers holding him back did not relinquish their hold.

The watermind that spoke previously knelt down by Jessii, looking at her face. "You well?" he asked.

Jessii nodded meekly, but cringed at the sight of the wound on her leg. Blood seeped through her shorts. The watermind nodded, then placed a hand on her thigh, staining his fingers with her blood. Jessii understood from his body language that his intentions were good, so she relaxed as much as she could.

He closed his eyes and water flowed from his palm. It soothed and rippled against her leg, mending the skin. Jessii pulled her shorts up, revealing only a scar. The young man cut her free from the rope, then nodded to the other men. They applied their own sets of wrist and ankle restraints on Braden and shoved him away from the tree.

"You boys don't know what you're-" Braden started to say.

Jessii had only a moment to act, so she took it, dashing to the side. Though as soon as she moved, the forest around her came to life. Snarls and growls echoed from within, and a second later a group of draks broke through the tree line, chomping their jaws and flashing their razor sharp teeth and claws.

The waterminds acted out of instinct, countering the draks with their water blasts. Jessii grabbed one of Braden's dropped knives and lowered herself into a defensive stance just as a drak barreled toward her, its paws outstretched to slice Jessii in half. She pushed off her leg, now healthy and eager for the challenge, and dodged the drak's strike. She cut the beast, entering a deadly bout. With every swipe she evaded and attacked. Draks were relentless, enraged beasts, and the key to defeating them was to stick to a plan. Dodge and strike. They could take quite a beating, but as long as Jessii stuck it out she'd emerge victorious.

"Ahh!" Braden cried.

Out of the corner of her eye, she saw another drak break past the waterminds, running straight for Braden. He was defenseless and restrained.

I should let you rot, she thought for a half second. It wouldn't be right though, and that was the difference between them.

Jessii evaded another slashing claw, then slammed Braden's knife down on the beast's paw. It cut clean through and into the tree root beneath it. A perfect hit. The beast wasn't dead, but at least it would leave her alone while she dealt with the other one.

You don't deserve this, shit-rat. Jessii leapt for the drak. She slammed her shoulder into the beast, throwing it off balance a split second before its jaws connected with Braden's neck. The drak shook off the blow but charged again. Jessii sidestepped each attack, then rolled toward where her blade lay against a rock. In one fluid motion, she unsheathed Sorya, sliced the beast's neck, and sheathed her again. Blood gurgled from the fallen creature, puddling at Braden's feet.

"That's really gross," he said, scurrying away from it.

Jessii peeked over her shoulder, the earlier drak just freed itself from the tree trunk, spewing blood from its paw. For a split second it looked at her, but then it rejoined its pack to fight the waterminds.

She looked down at Braden, scowling.

"Shall we be off, then?" he asked.

Jessii brought the tip of her blade down so that it poked his throat, then pulled him to his feet. She nodded toward camp.

"You got it, love."

*****

"Maybe we should just get back, Neema," Milo told her. "You've been thinking we were on their trail for a day now, and it's getting dark. We don't even know if the squad we're tailing is Tem's."

Neema didn't respond, but took note of Evan's silence on the matter. Now that he knew what they were doing out here he barely said a word. *Is it jealousy?* Neema asked herself. "Men…" She shook her head and continued hacking her way through the jungle.

"What do you-"

"Sh!" Neema interrupted Milo's fifth attempt at talking her back to camp. She held up her fist and turned her ear out to listen better. There was something there.

Neema snuck close to a bush to peer ahead. She gasped when she got a clear view.

A dozen draks, all dead, lay strewn about the area.

"What the hell happened here?" Evan whispered, looking for himself. "This is an entire pack. They would've slaughtered any of our squads."

Blood and remains carpeted the ground, and when Neema stepped closer, the ground squished underneath her feet. She looked down, then back to Milo and Evan.

"Waterminds."

Just then, leaves rustled nearby. Instantly, Neema grabbed her elemental rods set to earth and lightning, Milo engaged his gauntlets, and Evan racked his rifle. Neema's heart thrashed in her chest waiting for the threat to emerge.

A rabbit hopped from a bush and scampered away as it saw Neema and her squad. Neema relaxed her shoulders, freeing her pent-up breath.

Evan turned. "I think I hear-"

Before he could finish what he was saying, a wave smacked Neema so hard her world turned blue. She spun and twisted under the current, luckily maintaining control of one of her elemental rods.

Not again, she thought. This time, she tried blocking the water with a large chunk of rock she created with her earth rod, depleting the earth stone's power. "Shit!" she cursed. The ground squished beneath her feet, loosing her stance and dropping her to a knee. She caught a glimpse of her lightning rod and dove to the side, narrowly dodging another wave blast. She clawed through the mud, grasping the lightning rod and countering with an attack of her own. Through the splashes and sparks, she couldn't make out anything more than the silhouette of her attacker.

"Go!" she yelled, hoping that Milo and Evan knew what to do. Even if it wasn't Tem, the only way they could hope to defeat a mindless was by surrounding him.

"Hyaah!" she cried, attacking every wave like it were a game. By the end of it she was a sopping mess, sloshing around in the mud and sweat. Milo stood above the mindless soldier, and Evan from the other side a moment later.

"There was only one?" she asked herself out loud, regaining her breath.

"I saw two others, but they're dead. Draks got to em." Evan said.

Milo pointed to the unconscious watermind. "This one was too busy with you, so I came up beside him and laid him out cold. He probably won't be out long."

Neema nodded and looked down.

Is it?

She knelt down and flipped the soldier over. Immediately, she gasped. "Tem!"

"You're kidding," Milo said, kneeling next to her. "Well, I'll be… what are the chances of that?"

"We should hurry up and move," Evan said. He reached into his pack and grabbed a sedative. "No tellin if there are more mindless out there."

"Or draks…" Milo cautioned.

Neema nodded, letting her hand graze along Tem's cheek as she stood and let Evan administer the sedative.

"That should keep him under until we get him back to camp," Evan said.

Milo scooped Tem up in his arms, and in that moment, he looked as he did as a young boy. She caught a whiff of his scent, salty and woodsy, like driftwood at sea. Neema didn't realize she was smiling until she caught Milo watching her. She shook the expression from her face and started to grab her things from the mud.

"Hey, wait a sec!" Evan called out. Neema turned and found him a few meters away, bent over by a tree.

She crossed her arms in front of her chest without a word, waiting.

"Something happened here," he said, as if he were piecing something together in his head.

This time she responded, her impatience getting the best of her. "Yes, Evan. We've established that. Draks, mindless?" She waved at the bloody, muddy mess that surrounded them.

Evan shook his head. "No, not that. Jessii was here."

Neema leaned in closer, trying to see what he did. "How do you know?"

"She's heading that way," he said, pointing toward camp.

"Then let's go find her," Neema said.

Chapter Ten

It took them the rest of the night and multiple breaks, but they followed Jessii's trail all the way back to camp. They heard the commotion before breaking through the clearing. Braden shouted, his voice as excruciating as if Neema took Jessii's sword and clanked it against a rock a hundred times.

"Remove these restraints!" Braden cried. "I'm back, aren't I?"

Neema motioned for Milo to sneak around the side of camp with Tem. At least Braden was good enough to cause a distraction.

"Come on, Evan." He was already in front of her, his fists balled with little veins popping out of them.

Ah shit, Neema thought. Before she could catch up, Evan was inches from Braden's face.

"Woah! Evvy!" Braden said, trying to back away. "Your sister, man. She's got to learn some manners, I mean, look at-"

Before Braden could finish, Evan's hands were around his throat. "What did you do to her!?"

Jessii stood off to the side, her face an expressionless mask.

"Lock him up," Neema ordered.

"You don't have the authority!" Braden yelled as the guards seized him, tearing him from Evan's grasp. "You'll pay for this, Neema!"

"What's going on here?" Mezzy approached with two soldiers.

"All finished here, Mez," Neema said. "Braden is back, our shift is over, and I'm going to bed."

"What about you?" Mezzy asked Jessii. Mezzy tenderly reached out and stroked her shoulder. "Need any sort of attention? Medical or otherwise?"

Jessii flicked her eyes from Mezzy to Neema to Evan and then to the ground before smiling and shaking her head.

Mezzy whispered something else, but Neema couldn't make out what it was. *Is Jessii blushing?*

"What am I supposed to do with him?" Mezzy asked, jutting her thumb toward Braden.

Neema looked at both Jessii and Evan, hoping she gauged them correctly. Jessii didn't appear hurt, but there was something in her eyes that told Neema enough. "He deserted the rebellion and hurt one of my subordinates upon capture. I'm sure you can cook up a fitting punishment for him." Neema stalked off, grabbing Jessii's hand as she did and clapping Evan's shoulder. "We want the day off now, so don't bother us!" she called back without looking.

Neema didn't realize how fast she was walking, toting Jessii through camp back to the barracks. She barged through the door, and her eyes landed on her bunk where Tem lay unconscious.

"I need him up on this table," Milo said, moving bunks aside to make room for his workstation. Evan grabbed Tem from under his shoulders, and Neema grabbed his legs.

Jeez, he's heavy! Neema thought. They set him down, and Milo went straight to work. Jessii stood by, helping Milo hold different tools in place and adjust Tem's position when needed. Before long, Neema saw the water stone glow from Tem's neck.

"Do all of em have glowing skin like that?" Evan asked, pointing to the stone. "I've never seen a mindless so close before."

"Where's that collar, Neema?" Milo asked.

"Oh! Right." She sifted through her pack. While on patrol she had worked on it off and on. It took her half a spool of wiring, a dozen power chips, and two wind shards, but what she made, according to Milo, should create some type of barrier around Tem's stone, lessening the controlling effect on his mind.

Her hands shook as she handed the collar to Jessii, who helped Milo secure it around Tem's neck. Milo made it look easy, but a bead of sweat slowly fell from his brow, down his cheek and neck where it disappeared beneath his tank top.

Only when Milo stepped back and examined his work did Neema realize she was biting her cuticles.

"So?" she asked.

Milo shrugged his shoulders. "Seems right to me, but only one way to know for sure."

Neema nodded to Evan. "Wake him up."

Evan popped open a small container and shoved it under Tem's nose. In a few seconds, Tem's blazing, blue eyes opened.

He put his hand to head and rubbed his temples, then sat up, looking down at himself. Evan tensed and laid a hand on his rifle.

"Don't," Neema told him. Her eyes never left Tem, and when she spoke he looked up at her, studying her. It was as if he'd seen her for the very first time.

Tem opened his mouth. His voice cracked and croaked. He growled and coughed, putting his head down, then he looked back up at Neema.

"Neema?" he whispered. His eyes squinted, and he shook his head again like he struggled to remember or make the connection.

"It's working!" she said. "Yes, Tem. It's me!"

Milo's face still held caution as he hovered over Tem, placing a hand on his shoulder and looking into his eyes.

Tem looked at Milo's hand, and then at Milo. His eyes narrowed.

"It's okay, Tem." Neema said. "He's helping you."

Tem tugged at the collar around his neck.

"Ah ah!" Milo said. "Keep that thing secure. Don't want you going all crazy on us now."

"I remember things," Tem said to Neema. "I saw you." Tem shook his head like he was trying to rattle the memories to the surface. "The other night. You tried to talk to me."

Neema put her hand to her mouth. Milo already grabbed a notebook and began jotting down observations.

Neema walked over to Tem, kneeling over him. "And now I can."

Tem smiled. It was the same smile she remembered.

"Give us a minute," Neema told the others. Milo looked a little hurt at that. *He probably wants to keep recording Tem's progress.* Evan and Jessii cleared out without a word.

Tem leaned back and looked up, stretching his neck. "It's all hard to remember."

"It's okay. You're here now, and that's what matters." Just then Neema had an idea. She flicked her eyes to the back of the barracks. "You know what? There's somethin I wanna show you."

Neema grabbed Tem's hand, pulling him along with her. She

unhooked the lock and slid the two of them through the back to a rough patch of jungle.

Now's as good a time as any. And after all that patrolling, she might as well take advantage of her day off. As they walked, she felt eyes on her. Jessii sat on the roof of the barracks, dangling her legs over the edge. Neema held a finger to her lips. Jessii rolled her eyes in response, as if Neema and Tem were two kids running off to go play without their parents' permission.

"Where are we going?" Tem asked.

Neema looked back and smiled, "I'll show you." His cheeks were tinted with a splash of pink.

Is he blushing? she thought. Maybe this was her Tem. The tiny path she'd seen weeks ago was even smaller now, almost fully covered by growing vegetation. She ducked under and around prickly branches, peeking back at Tem every few steps.

"Not much farther!" she said, hoping she was right. The hike got her blood flowing, and the humid jungle just made it worse.

"You sure about that?" Tem asked.

When she thought they might have to turn back, the path opened to overlook a crescent shaped pond with two waterfalls, one flowing into the pond, and one pouring out to the ocean. The afternoon sun glittered down on it, setting the water ablaze with a thousand little dancing sparkles.

Tem joined her, and she heard the breath escape his mouth. "Wow."

She held his hand, clenching her jaw, because she knew that if she said anything, something more than words would come out. A hundred tears welled up in her eyes, threatening to break the emotional dam she so strongly fought to keep intact.

Okay, get a grip, Neema, she told herself. *How old are you anyway?*

Before she could think about her feelings anymore, Neema nudged him with her hip. "Come on." She hopped up to the high waterfall, stripping off her jacket, shirt, boots, and pants along the way. Looking back at Tem, she noticed his eyes were wider than the time he walked in on her wearing only a towel after she'd bathed.

"Watch this!" Neema launched herself from the side of the waterfall into the pool, flying twenty feet through the air before plunging into the deep cold. Goosebumps rippled across her body, but as she swam, they subsided. Neema whipped her hair around and looked over at Tem, standing up above on the rocks.

"Come on in!" she called.

He slid off his leather shoes, torn shirt, and pants. Neema floated backwards in the water, watching the sun glisten off his toned chest and arms.

You grew up, didn't you?

In less than a second, he skipped his way to the top of the waterfall. Watching him warmed Neema inside, despite the cold water. *You haven't lost your touch for climbing either.* With a familiar, toothy grin, Tem stepped over the edge, plummeting into the waterfall.

Neema almost cried out, but as Tem was about to hit the water he manipulated the waterfall, spreading it out before him in a gentle wave. He surfed it all the way to where Neema floated, the splashes rolling over her body.

"Showoff!" Neema said.

"You should talk!" Tem snickered. "I saw those sweet moves you pulled out."

As their eyes met, Tem's smile faded slightly. It was like he was settling into her gaze just as he lowered himself into the water.

"You don't need to do that," he said, nodding at how she bobbed up and down. Tem floated motionless.

Neema scoffed, "I can't control water like you. I kind of have to."

Tem floated closer. Neema could feel the pool tighten around her. "Woah!" she yelped.

"It's okay," Tem said. "You can trust me."

Neema stopped kicking her legs and arms to stay afloat, letting the water do it for her. Her breath caught in her lungs. It was something so simple, but it felt remarkable. She was walking on water.

"Now move," Tem said. He floated backwards in the water, watching her. Neema leaned forward, and the water kept her afloat beneath the ripples.

"Ha! This is amazing."

Tem held out his hand for her, and she reached out. All of a sudden, the water gave out beneath her and she fell beneath the surface. She screamed out a muffled gurgle. After a few kicks she returned to the surface where Tem had his head tipped back in laughter.

"You idiot!" she yelled. She splashed a handful of water at him, but it parted before it reached him. Tem held up a hand and the drops of water stayed in midair. He looked at her with a mischievous smile. "Don't you even think about it!"

As soon as she got the sentence out, he flicked his wrist and pushed the water right back at her. Neema dipped beneath the surface of the water and swam toward him, tackling him. They played, wrestling back and forth beneath the surface before Neema kicked away to rise and catch her breath.

She spun around, scanning the shoreline and ledges surrounding the pool. All was quiet above water.

"Tem?" she asked, wondering why he hadn't come up for air. "Tem!"

The water beneath her glowed right before the pool erupted, launching Tem high into the air. The water churned, suspending him in the air, and Neema felt the water beneath her lift her up to him.

He lowered his head, bringing his face inches from hers. "Now I want to show *you* something."

Neema raised an eyebrow. "No funny business this time?"

"Promise."

She took Tem's outstretched hand, and he lowered them back down, wrapping his arms around her. She reached around his neck, resting her chin in the soft area of his neck, breathing in his salty scent, and feeling the smoothness of his skin against hers.

Beneath the surface, they passed darting schools of fish. *How deep is this pool?* she wondered, getting her answer a moment later when the pool's floor lit up with coral, colorful seaweed, and neon, moss covered rocks. Tem flew her past it all to a cave tucked behind the waterfall.

Neema tugged on Tem's shoulder. She couldn't hold her breath much longer. He turned and pointed to the cave, but she responded by pointing at her mouth. Tem held Neema's neck and kissed her, filling her lungs with a fresh breath of air.

His lips lingered for a second, then he flew her into the cave. Neema tore her eyes away from Tem and looked forward. The walls were scarred from years and years of water pouring through, and a faint light grew stronger as they approached. When they rounded the corner Neema almost lost her breath again.

Pure water crystals jutted through the rocks below. They provided a bright green and blue hue that reflected off the walls within the cavern.

Wow, what is up with these fancy caves I keep getting brought to?

Neema crawled out of the water and laid down, breathing deep. Tem scooted next to her, their hips touching. A small, sandy beach glittered in the light of the crystals, surrounding the pool. It was barely large enough for the two of them.

Everything's glowing, she thought, looking around. The moss that covered the rocks, the crystals beneath the water, the plants that grew against the walls, and the sand that covered the beach. It was a beautiful hideaway, untouched by the rest of the world. Shades of greens and blue swirled in the water and onto the crescent moon beach.

"This is-" Neema started.

"Beautiful," Tem said. Neema could just make out the pupils within the blue storms in his eyes, and realized they were focused on her. If she were any other girl she would've blushed, but all she felt was her warming heart. The rest of her body remained cold and covered in goosebumps.

"I didn't know you could breathe underwater. Let alone breathe for me."

Tem chuckled. "Yeah, I should've warned you first."

"It's not like we haven't kissed before." Neema thought back to the first and only kiss they shared. The day Tem was taken from her. She'd wanted him to kiss her for months before that day, but when she finally got what she wanted her world twisted and cracked.

"A lot has changed since then," he said.

"A lot has stayed the same too." It was her this time who focused on him. The pink that swelled in his face only enhanced his almost white hair and blue eyes. Neema leaned forward and kissed him. His lips were soft and salty like the ocean, and his breath on her lips a warm summer breeze.

Neema pushed him back into the sand. She wrapped a leg around one of his and dug her hands into the sand like claws. It was then that he kissed her back, from her lips to her cheek and down to her neck. Neema grazed his chest with her hand. Bits of sand trailed off and fell on his tanned skin.

Tem's eyes flashed brighter for a moment, and he kissed her again. He ran his hand through her hair to the small of her back, and then she noticed that the tide rose.

"Oh!" she said. Her feet were slick with water, and it was getting higher with each kiss.

"It's okay," he said. As she turned, she realized it wasn't the tide. Tem was controlling the surrounding water, and he used it to massage and caress her. The water's grip was firm, like Tem's own.

"I've missed you," Neema said. She untied the knot in her bra and let it slip away to the sand.

"You're all that made me remember who I was," Tem said in between kisses. "It was like being a prisoner in my own body."

Listening to his words made Neema's heart flutter like a dozen hummingbirds swarming around a garden. She couldn't find the words to tell him he was what kept her going all these years, chipping away at the king's infrastructure to find *him*.

And here he was. All hers.

Hands made of water clutched her butt, her hips, her abdomen, sliding over her navel before cupping her breasts. A fire ignited deep within her, and Tem fanned the flames. She needed him. *All* of him.

She reached down and slipped his under clothes free. "You're not trapped anymore."

Tem's eyes met hers. Those shimmering sapphires, wide with lust. His excitement rose beneath her, and a wave of water curled over them. She slipped her underwear off and straddled him, guiding him inside her.

For the first time in five years, she was whole.

This is perfect, she thought as they tangled and intertwined on the sand, in the pool, then back to the sand. Tem's eagerness to please her showed, even if it took him a couple of tries figuring it out. As the night continued, she was clawing at the sand, arching her back, and writhing beneath him.

She couldn't tell how long they'd been there, but sweat beaded on her chest and sand clung to her hair, body, and in between her toes.

Can this night never end? she thought, resting her head on Tem's chest. His steady breathing lulled her toward a blissful sleep. *I think I deserve that much.*

By Antonio Baldari

*****

"We should get back before they worry," Neema said, stretching across Tem's chest.

"Do we have to?" he asked, yawning.

She smiled. "No, but I should go check in. Plus, we gotta find you some clothes. Those rags you wore in will *not* do."

Tem scoffed, but stood up. "I'm surprised you're a part of all this. The rebellion that is."

"Really?"

"It's a fool's errand. You've done good by me, but nothing will stop the king. He's too powerful."

"How does he do it? Control all of you?"

Tem looked into the water and sighed. There was no way he'd know the answer. Only the king would.

Tem's eyes squinted, and he cocked his head to the side. "You're right, I think we should go."

Neema grabbed his hand. "Is something wrong?"

"I don't know," he said, lowering himself into the pool. Judging by the crinkle in his brow, she had to bet something wasn't right. She took his hand, and he swam them back. What was a bright and cheery blue now turned almost pitch black. She couldn't see anything in the water other than bits of moss that glowed as they swam by. When they reached the surface, sounds of war filled the night.

"Oh no, this can't be happening!" Neema said. Tem brought her to shore, and she was shivering before she made it to her clothes. She hurriedly threw them on and started running back to camp with Tem on her heels.

This couldn't be any worse, she thought. *I'm dripping wet, half-naked, and there's sand in my ass! Someone's going to pay!*

As they bolted through the path, the camp appeared over the next rise. There *was* a war. A legion of mindless soldiers of every element attacked the rebels.

"They don't stand a chance," she muttered, her shoulders sagging. They arrived at the barracks, bursting through the door, but no one was there. When she turned to leave, she caught movement from within, so she spun, ready to attack.

"You betrayed us." The voice was familiar, but raspy like it was drug across sandpaper before leaving his lips. "Or rather, *he* betrayed us, love."

Braden emerged from the shadows, pointing a shaky finger at Tem. He grasped one of Neema's elemental rods, activating its lightning stone.

"Don't even-" Before Neema finished Braden swung.

Damn, he's fast!

Tem pulled her out of the way, but the lightning rod caught him, singeing his shoulder.

Braden brought out Neema's other rod, set to fire.

"Bastard!" she yelled. "Give those *back*!"

Outside the barracks, explosions, gunfire, and agonizing cries thundered like a terrible storm.

We don't have any time! It wouldn't be much longer until the camp was destroyed. *The rebellion will be destroyed...*

"Stop!" Neema yelled at Tem and Braden, but they wouldn't listen.

Neema ran at Braden. His eyes were wild and dangerous. He swung at her, but she dodged and wrapped his arm up to yank her fire rod back.

They exchanged blows, countering and parrying back and forth. Just as Braden was about to get the upper hand, Tem got in the way. A shower of sparks, water, and flame erupted.

When the chaos cleared, Tem and Braden were both on the ground and half the building was gone.

"Neema!" someone shouted.

Neema couldn't answer, she had to see to Tem. He was lying on the ground as still as the moon above.

"Tem!" she cried. "Tem!" She looked down at the collar around his neck. *Something's wrong...*

"The chips dislodged," Milo said, appearing beside her. He was right, Neema needed to get them set before-

Tem's body was cold. *Ice* cold. Neema flinched and retracted her arm, then leaned forward to get a better look.

"Can you fix it?" she asked.

"There's no time, Neema."

She shoved Milo away and reached over Tem, searching the back of his neck for the elemental stones. Ice crystallized around Tem's neck and began covering his body.

"No! No no no no no!" She kept trying to work at it, but the ice was so cold it burned. Tem looked like he'd been sitting in a snowstorm for a month.

The war thundering around them was at their feet, held back by Evan and Jessii.

"Let's go, Neema!" Milo said, grabbing her by the shoulders.

"No wait!" she yelled. "Tem!"

Tem's eyes opened suddenly. They were pure white.

"No... it can't be."

He didn't turn to look at her. He merely sat up and looked at his arms, his body, and then felt at the wound in his neck. His body color returned to normal, the ice falling off in slushes.

"Neema…" Milo started, tightening his hold on her.

It was just like her dream. Tem looked up at her with unknowing eyes. He began to yell and struggle with himself.

"You can fight it, Tem!" she yelled. Milo lifted her up and slung her over his shoulder. Evan and Jessii were there too. They all began to run, but Neema kept struggling, kicking, fighting for a way back to Tem. He wouldn't be taken from her again. Not again!

The mindless swarmed Tem, but others pursued Neema's squad. Tem's scream was still ringing in her ears. Then the cold left. The air began to sizzle and crack, and all the mindless turned their attention away from her squad. A deafening roar cut through the night. Milo set Neema down, and they all turned. The yurdrak had arrived.

Chapter Eleven

Neema wiped the tears from her eyes as she craned her neck to look at the creature.

"Is that... lava?"

Fire and earth melted together all over the yurdrak, and molten lava dropped from its skin like sludge. The beast stood for a moment, its burning, orange eyes watching all the mindless and rebels inside the camp.

The mindless army made the first move, but the yurdrak blasted lava at the first wave. They disappeared in a whiff of steam.

"They don't stand a chance," Milo said.

"We're getting out of here!" Evan said. Milo and Jessii nodded, but Neema looked back toward Tem.

"Go," Neema said. "I'll catch up!"

"Neema..." Milo said, shaking his head.

"*GO!*"

She wouldn't let them risk their lives for Tem. They'd done more than they should have already. As she turned away from them, she stopped dead. Tem was standing up with his emotionless eyes fixed on the yurdrak. *No,* she thought. *Tem, don't! You'll die!*

She tried to run, but a freezing wind forced her to the ground, biting into the yurdrak's heat.

"Tem?" Water and wind swirled and spun beneath and around him, faster and faster until it slowed, turning into ice. Tem erupted from its center, donning armor made from the ice he created. In one massive gust of wind, he flew directly toward the yurdrak.

The yurdrak spewed lava, but Tem blocked it with a shield of ice, then launched a spear at the monster. It melted as it hit the beast's armor-like skin. A paw the size of a house slammed to the ground, and spikes of steaming rock jutted out, killing dozens of rebels and mindless alike.

Neema watched in awe, realizing this was beyond anything within her capabilities. *I'm powerless,* she thought. *The only thing I'll do here is get Tem killed.*

It tore at her, knowing his best chance at living was without her. She looked up to the sky where he fought with the monster. Lightning strikes from other mindless reflected off a huge ice sword Tem brandished, and a storm raged further above. Every time Tem clashed with the beast ice and molten rock showered the camp.

Something Braden said triggered in her mind as she watched Tem fight. *He betrayed us.* Tem couldn't be the cause for all this, could he? *Then why did he say the rebellion was so foolish?*

"I gotta get outta here," she whispered as a sizzling boulder demolished the remains of her barracks.

She turned and made out the glint of Jessii's sword fading in the distance. If she left now, she could catch up quickly.

I have to let you go, Tem, but I will find you again, she vowed.

He couldn't have been the cause for the mindless attack. It was still the same old Tem she knew from before, right?

She saw the shadow but couldn't do anything to prevent what happened next. Whatever struck the back of Neema's skull made it feel like it had split in two. Everything went dark before she even hit the ground.

When she awoke, her eyes had to adjust to the light. Her head throbbing with pain was barely a faint memory, but she knew it hadn't been that long since she was struck.

"Wait, what?" she said, looking around her. It was the same cave she woke up in before. There was a pool of bathing water, the same pit of fire, and the same rock formations.

"Who's there?" she asked, feeling the presence of someone else with her. Whatever it was watched her, hidden and camouflaged.

She sat up quickly to move, but something held her back. She'd felt this before, something controlled the wind surrounding her, keeping her seated.

"It's okay, little one," a deep, gravelly voice spoke. "My name is Sizaal, and I've come to help you."

The creature stirred slightly in the corner, just enough for Neema to make out the branches, rocks, and elements that created its body.

Neema didn't know what to say, but she choked out the first thing she thought of. "Where's Tem?"

"I may answer your questions soon, young one. First, you will answer mine." Sizaal held up her elemental rod. "Why do you create such a weapon? If the intent is to kill, why kill? Why do you kill, small one?"

"I have to save the ones I love."

"The ones…" Sizaal thought for a moment. "I see. I've been watching you for some time."

"What? How?"

Sizaal held up what she thought was its hand. "You carry special traits, *admirable* traits."

"And!?" Neema couldn't make sense of anything it was saying. "What the hell *are* you?"

"Ahh," Sizaal said. "That is a good question. A very good question. What is your desire, Neema?"

"You know my name? Alright, this is enou-"

"Silence!" the creature boomed. Neema's eyes went wide. Killing her would be an afterthought to a creature like this. "The world is at stake. Your petty qualms could have costly repercussions."

After a tense moment Neema nodded.

"Apologies. I get upset easily. My kind has not been treated well."

"I don't understand, Sizaal. I need you to tell me what's happening."

"No, I must *show* you." Sizaal stood. The creature was three feet taller than Milo and had eyes that changed color when he blinked. "Come." Sizaal extended a hand and the cave walls folded inward.

Neema's breath caught. Sizaal's control of the earth element was far greater than any other mindless she'd seen.

"You have questions," it said as they walked. "I am different from those abominations you call the mindless."

"Those *abominations* don't have a choice! You-"

"Follow a king that is not really a king, but a *thief* of the worst kind!"

"We must stop him!" Neema said.

"We must st-" Sizaal's words fell short. His eyes narrowed to crackling sparks. "You wish to stop the king?"

"That's what I've been trying to tell you!"

"Hmm." Sizaal nodded, then continued creating a path through the rocks until it opened to a brilliantly bright cavern.

Crystals of every element lined the walls, and a stream as colorful as a rainbow flowed alongside one of the walls.

"These-"

"Are not to be touched," Sizaal completed her sentence. "This place is sacred."

He continued while they walked, "What you call a yurdrak has evolved into something the world hasn't witnessed in ages, your people would now call it a *yurdrakon*. It possesses control of two powerful elements. Its power is greater than can be imagined, and the last time one walked the world it left it in ruin."

"And how am I supposed to stop that thing? I don't think my rods would even make a dent."

"No, they wouldn't," Sizaal shook his moss covered head. "Which is why I need you to enter this cave and speak with the guardstone. It will know what to do." Sizaal gestured to a small, unnoticed cave that was completely dark amongst the bright, shining lights of the crystal-lit cavern.

"Why would I want to do something like that? Why should I help you end your conflict with the king?"

Sizaal turned his head, like the answer was obvious. "Because I will cure your lover of his affliction."

Neema knotted her eyebrows, but her chest fluttered. There was no cure. Tem would always be that way, and even if he did come back to her like before he would just turn again. The stone's power on his mind was too strong. "How? It's not possible."

"I've done many things you would term *impossible*. Hurry, little one, the guardstone awaits, and I must leave now if I am to save Tem, your love."

Neema looked toward the cave. Had it gotten darker? "What is the *guardstone*?" She turned back to Sizaal, but he was gone. Neema shook her head, "Yeah, great talk."

The cavern glittered and sparkled, but it was like the dark cave ahead sucked away any of that light.

"Here's goes nothin." Neema walked toward it, careful not to touch any of the crystals. As soon as she stepped in, the darkness swallowed her. A small, pulsing light floated up ahead, as if to guide her. It bobbed, weaving back and forth and leading her down, down, down. The light pulsed faster and stronger the further she went, and just as it looked to be on the edge of exploding, it darted around a bend.

The tunnel opened to a cavern the same size as the one prior, but it housed a single crystal that towered over Neema. It swirled dark blues and purples, and within its crevices it looked like an entire star system shone through. It lit the room with a dim but powerful light.

"Woah," Neema whispered. She reached out with a hand toward the crystal. The power this crystal must contain would be immense. *World changing.*

"Do not."

Neema jolted, her arm outstretched and inches away from the crystal. Where had the voice come from? Who had spoken? It didn't sound like it came from inside the cave.

"I am here... and most places."

"Where?" Neema said under her breath. She knew then, the voice didn't come from anywhere in the cavern. It was inside her mind.

"You know already," the voice said. "I am Arlac, the final guardstone." The crystal in front of her shimmered slightly, as if nodding

155

to her in introduction.

"I'm Neema."

"I know who you are, and what you intend to do. You will fail, but with my help you may succeed. Your judgment is too skewed, your knowledge clouded. I will show you the truth." The guardstone began to glow from deep within. A rhythm started to pulse in her head. It got brighter and louder within seconds. Neema almost cried out for it to stop before Arlac radiated the most magnificent light. When the light washed away, she was somewhere else.

The sun shone overhead, reflecting off clear blue water. White foam massaged the sand stretching up and down the coast. Behind her was a temple adorned with jewels of every color and plated in gold. Each corner of its roof curled, as if the sky wished to tug it off and peak within.

"Go inside," Arlac told her. There was no sign of the guardstone, but its presence in her mind remained.

Neema walked up the steps to the temple, noting the sparkling moat that surrounded it. Her steps made no sound, and as she approached, the water receded, revealing steppingstones to lead her to the temple doors. The doors opened, and sunlight beamed inside, but it wasn't needed. Three guardstones stood at the far end of the temple, all of them shining with an intensity that filled the building.

"I thought you were the only one left?" she said.

Arlac's voice in her head spoke, its tone somber. "I am. This is but a memory."

As soon as Arlac finished speaking, the door behind her slammed shut. She turned and a large creature that looked like Sizaal rode in on top of a drak. The creature wore gleaming, golden armor, adorned with jewels. It hopped off of the drak and stomped toward the guardstones.

Neema didn't notice before, but there was another creature bent on one knee in front of the guardstones. The creature rose and turned to her. He looked different, younger, but she still recognized Sizaal.

"They are called sanctors. They served us in the time before."

Neema thought the question, but never asked it. Knowing Arlac could read her thoughts unnerved her.

"I won't dig further into your thoughts than is required. Your privacy is yours."

Neema blushed as she thought about Tem, and wondered how far into her thoughts Arlac would go.

"When you're done thinking about your man lover, you should pay attention to the conversation before you." Arlac said it in a playful tone, and Neema blushed further. She returned her attention to the scene in front of her. Sizaal was trying to calm the other sanctor, but wasn't having any effect.

"You can't disgrace the guardstones with this nonsense, Pra'tear!"

"They disgrace *us*, brother! They give gifts to these pathetic humans, while we bend and scrape at their base! I will do it no more!"

"SILENCE." The voice boomed inside Neema's mind. It wasn't Arlac's voice. This one didn't sound as old, or as kind.

"You demand silence only when I speak the truth!" Pra'tear pushed past Sizaal to the guardstone in the center of the room. The guardstone swirled with light faster than before. Neema could feel its immense energy swelling.

"You don't know what you speak," Sizaal said.

"I've learned the truth, guardstone," Pra'tear said, ignoring Sizaal. He jabbed a finger. "You can't control me anymore."

Pra'tear opened his other hand to reveal a stone, darker than the darkest night and surrounded by white flame. Neema sensed the tension in the room rise beyond boiling.

"He has the eclipse stone!" one of the guardstones, a feminine presence, said.

A shadow fell outside the temple, and Pra'tear extended his arm. The stone formed into a sword.

"OBEY!" the center guardstone yelled, but Pra'tear had already swung. A flash of light streaked across the temple, and in the next instant the guardstone cracked and went dark. It's presence gone. Destroyed.

The air in the temple stilled for only a moment, and then pure chaos ensued. Sizaal lunged for Pra'tear, but got knocked straight into the door behind Neema. Another guardstone rippled with power, blasting pure energy at Pra'tear. The shining white sword Pra'tear wielded absorbed the energy, as if it fed on it.

"No!" the guardstone yelled. "The Essence has no effect. Arlac! Take the sanctor! I can't hold him!"

The light in the temple shifted. Neema understood she wasn't there, so she walked the aisle of the temple to where Pra'tear inched toward the guardstone.

"Re'la!" Arlac yelled. "You can make it! Join us!"

The ground shook, and the walls wavered. Parts of the ceiling started to come down. Neema studied Pra'tear. There were certain features of him that looked familiar, but she couldn't place from where.

He knelt and rummaged through the broken crystals of the destroyed guardstone. Underneath it was a single black bead. Pra'tear picked it up and rolled it in his fingers. The air around Arlac darkened, and the image distorted. It was like another place was wrapping itself around it. Sizaal as well.

Pra'tear laughed. "You can run, guardstone, but in the end *you* will serve *me*. *All* will serve me! And with what I now know I will rule forever! So run! Hide! *Fear* me and watch as I turn your precious humans into my slaves!"

He pulled apart the rocks and branches that made up his chest to reveal five glowing hearts. Neema knew they were elements. He placed the bead in between all of them, and she watched as every element merged into one.

"Essence," Neema said.

"Yes," Arlac told her. "*Absolute* Essence."

"You will not!" Re'la cried. "Go Arlac! Now!"

A massive blast of energy shot from the guardstone to Pra'tear, ripping away the eclipse sword. The temple walls tore like paper and the skies outside darkened.

Arlac was already somewhere else with Sizaal, watching from a distance but still only a few feet away. Arlac spoke, "You have fallen, Pra'tear, and you will be cursed for it. You may have ultimate power, but I will not grant you free rein of it!"

A heavy, burdening energy weighed Pra'tear to his knees, ripping away the rocks and branches that made up his body. What was torn away regrew almost immediately, but as flesh and blood. Pra'tear's face contorted, slowly transforming to that of a human.

Neema peered closer, "It can't be."

"You will be bound to the humans you hate so much, Pra'tear," Arlac said. "One day I will find a way to reverse what you've done. The power you've stolen will return to where it belongs."

"I will live forever, guardstone, and I will find you. I will rip your bond of me free if it's the last thing I do." The man stood, his naked body almost glowing from the Essence held within it. He watched Arlac and Sizaal leave with a menacing smile.

The viewing portal around Arlac closed, and with it the vision faded. Neema still had the image of Pra'tear's face clear in her mind.

Neema opened her eyes, and she was back in the cavern with Arlac. As soon as she caught a breath, stars dazed in her eyes and her limbs went weak.

"Pra'tear is the king."

Chapter Twelve

Jessii stood at the ridge, looking out across the country.

What was that? she thought. Something about the world *shifted*. She listened, the breeze could tell a lot if one merely paid attention.

That doesn't make sense, she thought, trying to decipher the elements around her. It was like trying to understand someone speaking in a different dialect.

Something had changed. She couldn't tell what it was, and she wasn't sure if she liked it. Times were hard enough. There were maybe a couple dozen survivors from the attack.

Jessii looked back, watching Mezzy delegate camp duties. Her fiery, red hair was noticeable even from a distance, and Jessii had to pull her eyes away to keep from staring. Since the attack, Mezzy was the only remaining superior in the rebellion, and she appointed Evan as her second in command.

Mezzy called Evan over, and though he did his best not to show it, Jessii noticed the slight trembling in his hands and the way he fidgeted when speaking with her.

Good, she thought. *We all should be scared.* If the elements were any indication, something bad was going to happen.

Jessii turned away and kept watch at the ridge, looking for any signs that they were followed.

No one will sneak up on us on my watch, Jessi told herself, keeping a hand on the hilt of her sword. Footsteps approached from behind. They were light enough that others wouldn't notice them, but Jessii's keen ear picked up on them right away.

"Been out here long?" Mezzy asked. Jessii eased her grip on her sword, surprised to see Mezzy away from camp. Lines and dark shadows spread from underneath Mezzy's eyes, but she still smiled as she sat next to Jessii on a rock overlooking the valley.

Jessii shrugged.

"I hear ya, or, I guess see ya would be more appropriate." Mezzy chuckled.

Jessii nodded up at Mezzy and bowed her head as if to ask how Mezzy was doing.

Mezzy sighed. "It's hard, ya know? How did we let this happen?" Jessii twitched her mouth.

"I guess it was bound to. Who are we against the might of the king?" Mezzy hung her head. Just then, it was like the shadows beneath her eyes spread to the rest of her body. Her shoulders hung a little lower and her breath shook.

Jessii wasn't sure if it was right, but it was like her body compelled itself to move. She reached out and grazed her hand against Mezzy's cheek. Mezzy looked up, and they stared into each other's eyes. Gray speckles mixed in with hazel.

"Your eyes are really pretty," Mezzy said, her voice full of breath. "I've noticed them before, but never this close."

Mezzy's gaze fell to Jessii's lips, making her heart quiver.

Does she want me to kiss her? Jessii asked herself, suddenly self-conscious of her scratchy, chapped lips. It would feel *amazing* to kiss her. *Wouldn't that scare her away though?*

"Say…" Mezzy said. "I've gotta run, but if you ever want someone to talk to, or if you wanna sit and listen to me question myself… my tent's open for you." Mezzy laid her hand on Jessii's upper thigh, and everything inside Jessii's body warmed at the touch.

Jessii nodded, squeezing her lips together as Mezzy got up and started back to camp. She scooted around on the rock, scrunched up into a ball, and watched Mezzy walk away. After a few feet, Mezzy stopped.

With her hand on her turned out hip, she flipped her hair back. "I hope you'll come by." Then she winked.

Jessii's blood raced through her veins. *Maybe we have more in common than I thought.*

*****

Neema was lost. Darkness surrounded her, but gleams of light swished by. There were reds and yellows, greens and blues, and colors Neema didn't know existed. The lights halted, like they just realized she was present and began to take an interest in her, wherever she was. Then a chain of violet light wrapped around her wrist. It burned for an instant, but there was no steam, no mark, and no lasting pain.

I can't move, she thought. A pool of golden light crawled up her leg. Another trickled down her arm. Her belly was covered in an orange glow. Every color attached itself to her body. Even her hair turned to radiant blue strands of light.

These are strands of Essence, she somehow knew. *They're so pure.*

163

"Yes," Arlac's presence returned, though she could feel it fading. "Essence is raw elemental power. As it gathers, it eventually forms into the crystals you've seen in my chamber and around the world."

The strands covered her completely, each one buzzing with power. They were in unison, yet Neema knew that each was entirely different. *This feels* good*!*

Then the lights dug, burrowing themselves inside her. The pain was overwhelming, and Neema screamed, though no noise escaped her lips. It lasted what felt like hours, each light delving deeper and deeper until they reached her very core. There, they converted into a single, absolute source of Essence. Then it was over, like it happened in the span of a breath.

She felt as she did before, alone in the darkness, but deep within her something was different.

"You have been given all that is left of me*,* " Arlac said. "Use these gifts to defeat Pra'tear. I am bestowing this power to you, because I believe you will make the right decision when the time comes. Don't choose as unwisely as Pra'tear did, Neema."

"Wait!" Neema called. She could feel the presence in her mind fading. "What decision? I don't understand! Why me!?"

She looked down and saw that she held a simple stone as dark as night but surrounded by the brightest day. *This is…* she thought for a moment, feeling the stone's energy. *The sun? And the moon?* She carefully put the stone in her pocket. *Not sure what you are, but I'll have to keep you safe.*

"Wow," she said, feeling the energy that pulsed inside her. "I understand now." She took a breath and felt every bit of air fill her chest, every ounce of blood rushing through her veins, and every spark of electricity at a new thought. She widened that awareness, perceiving the world around her. Every element was within her at all times. She didn't merely have control over them. She *was* every element. There were elements she didn't even know existed until this moment. They were everywhere, and everything. "It's beautiful."

She dug deeper into that understanding. "There's… a balance." Pra'tear abused that balance for his own pleasure. He needed to be stopped. He enslaved humanity so he could rule. Stole children to die for him. Left families broken for his amusement.

"I'm going to make you pay."

*****

Sizaal travelled through the forest, whizzing by trees and rocks like they were thrown at him.

I felt the boy's presence recently, he thought. *I must reach him before he disappears again!*

Tem flew by wind, setting a grueling pace for Sizaal to match. The other abominations stayed close, making it hard for Sizaal to seize any opportunity to capture the young man.

"Time is not on my side," Sizaal said. "The boy mustn't cause any more damage to the world! It is my duty to protect…"

Up ahead, the forest broke away to a lake. A river flowed from the mountain to the lake, then ran all the way to the sea, right next to Essence City.

"Something is wrong." He stopped. For the first time in a long while Sizaal was astounded. The entire lake was gone. It was replaced by pockets of lava in an otherwise dried up hole in the ground. "The yurdrakon did this."

He placed one hand on the ground, closing his eyes and *feeling* the world around him.

"It *was* here… ah! And what luck I have." On the other side of the lake, Tem knelt, as if mirroring Sizaal.

I would apologize for what I'm about to do to you, boy, but you will thank me for it.

Years, months, even days ago, Sizaal would not have relished battling with a master of wind and water. But he learned something recently. "The old Language still has power in this world."

With a burst of his earth heart, he transferred himself across the lake to where the boy waited. Without hesitation, Tem gathered dozens of razor sharp ice blades, all aimed at Sizaal.

In an otherworldly motion, Sizaal Said, "BIND!"

Tem's ice fell to a steaming puddle, and the boy froze in place.

Sizaal approached. "I promised Neema I would bring you to her," he told the boy as he wrapped him in a cocoon. "That is what I intend to do."

*****

Neema woke up on the ground, feeling as if she'd experienced the most vivid dream.

"Arlac?" She looked up at the guardstone, but the presence within the crystal was gone forever. Instead, she felt the intense Essence coursing through her body. "It was real," she told herself.

She rose to her feet, though she didn't feel as if she used her muscles to do so. Instead, the air around her lifted her up.

"Woah…" she said, gently landing back on the ground. Flames jumped from her palms and lightning sparked from her fingers, but those were mere strands in a web of elements heeding her call.

"I'll beat him," she said. With this power she could free Tem, her family, her friends. "And bring balance to this world."

"So, it's done." The deep voice behind Neema was unmistakable.

She growled, "Pra'tear." She didn't need to turn to know he was there, but she found it unnerving that he was able to sneak up on her. She felt *everything.* How could she not sense his presence until he was on top of her?

"I've been waiting for the day Arlac would pass his gift to another."

"You've abused your power," Neema replied. "It ends now."

She turned to face him. His human features were similar to when he was a sanctor. He had hair as dark as a sullen cloud, and a beard peppered with gray. Most would find him handsome, though Neema couldn't see past the evil that shrouded him.

"No." Pra'tear shook his head. "It doesn't." The king walked in a circle around her. "It will end when I tear the life stone from the corpse of the yurdrakon." He took a deep breath and shook as he continued. "I can feel it, can't you? Its power is… *intoxicating.*"

"I won't let you do that." Neema didn't know what the life stone was, but if it helped Pra'tear there was no way she could let him get to it.

"You won't have a choice. You see, I've been waiting for the day that Arlac transferred its Essence to another." His words crawled down her spine. "I can't kill you, yet, but I *can* bind you."

Neema was too late. She felt it just as Pra'tear's words drifted to her ears. Everything around her stilled. She couldn't move.

"In the coming eclipse, I will retrieve the life stone and return. Then I will take your Essence and kill you. I will rule for eternity as a *god*, and rid myself of this pathetic *human* form your guardstone cursed me with." His words were filled with such malice.

The king turned, his dark cape billowing behind him, and disappeared into the rock, leaving Neema alone in the darkness, full of power but with no way to use it.

Chapter Thirteen

The wind brought forth a warmth that forced Jessii to remove her shawl.

It's after dark and still unbearably hot, she thought.

The mindless were still behind them, but gaining. Mezzy tried to lead them east into the mountains, but a contingent of mindless cut off their path. South toward Essence City was their only option.

The clouds thickened, as they usually did above Essence City, masking the precious stars above. Jessii knew there was something wrong with the city. It didn't follow the rules of the world, and for that it was cursed to never see the sun. Tolerating the place as long as she and Evan did was enough.

And here I am, heading back to that cursed place.

Jessii sat on a spare log next to the campfire. Bits of ember flew in the air and were carried off in the wind's embrace. The elements had been in a constant state of intimacy and betrayal.

"Mezzy won't tell me what, but she's got a plan," Evan said. "I think it may be a secret weapon to put an end to all this. The yurdraks, mindless, everything."

"There's no such weapon! Why wait until *now* to use it?" Milo asked.

Jessii listened to the two bicker about Mezzy's plan. Every time they said Mezzy's name, Jessii stirred. She tried crossing her legs, biting her lip, and balling her fists to keep from feeling the way she did, but it didn't help. Mezzy's tent was right there in the corner of her eye, taunting her as much as the sound of her name.

Feeling as naked and exposed as ever, Jessii stood and walked away from the fire. She hoped Evan and Milo wouldn't notice her absence, each step feeling like it reverberated through camp.

What am I doing?

Light flickered within Mezzy's tent, but Jessii couldn't see anything through the tiny slit. With a courage she didn't realize she had, she slipped inside.

A lantern on top of a crate outlined Mezzy in orange as she bent over a desk looking at a map. She'd ditched her jacket and wore a pair of camo cargo pants that sat low on her hips, the sight making Jessii's insides tumble.

I have to be strong.

With one more ounce of nerve, Jessii tapped her foot on the ground.

"Oh!" Mezzy said, appearing startled. She leaned against the desk. "Hey there, stranger."

Jessii nodded.

"I'm just going over our route. Gotta stay one step ahead of those damned mindless." Mezzy gestured to her cot. "You can have a seat if you'd like. My tent isn't much, but I get a few perks for being in charge."

Jessii sat down and ran her hands down her thighs to her knees.

"Drink?" Mezzy sipped a dark liquid, then offered the glass to Jessii. Normally, Jessii turned down anything but water and tea, but tonight she made an exception.

The spiced liquor burned going down, but left a nice flavor in her mouth.

"Not bad, right? Better than the piss the men out there drink." As Mezzy set the glass on her desk, Jessii noticed fresh scars on Mezzy's back. She frowned and motioned to them when Mezzy turned back around.

"Oh, these? They're nothing. Got a little scraped up when one of those mindless launched me across camp."

Right when Mezzy sat down, Jessii smacked one of the gashes and watched as Mezzy curled her spine, crying in pain. "What the hell!?"

Jessii raised her eyebrows, contesting Mezzy's bravado.

Mezzy seethed. "Okay fine, they hurt! Happy?"

Jessii skittered around the cot so she sat behind Mezzy, and grabbed the nearby medical kit. She rubbed ointment on Mezzy's back, massaging her knotted muscles at the same time.

"Your hands are magical," Mezzy said, rolling her head like it was on a swivel.

Jessii sought out Mezzy's body rhythm, fine-tuning her own to match as she kneaded, mended, and caressed. She taped the cuts so they wouldn't get infected, then continued exploring Mezzy's bare skin inch by inch, learning as much about herself on the journey as she did about Mezzy.

Is this what I've been missing? she thought.

As Jessii's travels came to an end, Mezzy wrapped Jessii's arms around her, wearing her like a scarf.

Jessii was all too aware of how close their faces were.

I could kiss her right now. Should I?

As if Mezzy heard her thoughts, she said, "It's okay. You're still figuring it out. I can help you… if you want."

Jessii's body surged, filling with desire. She'd been waiting her whole life for someone to understand even a tiny portion of her. That feeling overwhelmed Jessii's senses, replacing them with a hunger she wasn't sure how to fulfill. She nodded.

"I know what it's like," Mezzy said while kissing Jessii's neck, "to be different. To hide. Maybe even be ashamed."

The breaths Jessii took were deep, heavy, and punctuated. Every time Mezzy kissed her it was like she was ballooning with energy, and at any moment she would burst.

"You just have to listen to your heart," Mezzy said, pulling down Jessii's shirt strap. "What's it telling you, Jessii?"

Jessii was about to melt into Mezzy's words, lips, and embrace when a commotion outside shook them both from their trance.

"Ah, hell," Mezzy cursed. "What now?" She rested her head on Jessii's chest, like she could escape from the world there, then grabbed her jacket. "S'pose I should see what all the hubbub is about. Promise we'll finish this later though."

Jessii adjusted her shirt, brushed her hair from her eyes, and bowed.

Mezzy almost turned to leave, but stopped short, then dashed back, descending on Jessii's lips. Their sweet, sticky embrace consumed Jessii, as did the way Mezzy's breath smelled like freshly torn mint leaves. Jessii ached for more, but in her next heartbeat it was over.

Woah, she thought. *I feel so… alive!*

Mezzy disappeared through the tent flap to the surrounding darkness. Jessii sat on the cot, cherishing the moment they shared and replaying it in her mind in vivid detail. Perhaps the world hadn't completely cursed her after all.

The tent flap opened, and Jessii inhaled, hoping to see Mezzy return. She huffed when she realized it was nothing but the wind.

Wait... The wind Spoke, and as soon as Jessii was able to decipher its message she hurried from the tent, her sword in hand. *I'm sorry, Mezzy. I've got to go!*

Jessii wished to be in her embrace again. To run her fingers through Mezzy's beautiful, red hair. To kiss her lips again and hold her closer and closer until they became one.

If she could live through the night, she might have that chance.

*****

Sizaal knew he would cause a commotion, as the first human that saw him fainted. The second cried, and the third swung a giant axe, almost chopping off a stray branch from his arm. After shouts and squalls from the little humans, they finally calmed down to the point that their leader invited him to their campfire to speak with her and her trusted advisors.

"Thank you for your *warm* invitation, leader Mezzy." Sizaal remained proper.

"And you are?" Mezzy asked.

"My name is Sizaal. I am the sanctor of the royal palace of the guardstones. Or at least I was. Now I travel in search of a way to defeat my enemy, Pra'tear, your king." Sizaal let that settle, and then added, "I am an acquaintance of the little one you call Neema. She is seeking assistance from the last guardstone, Arlac, as we speak, and should be joining us momentarily."

"And what are *you* doing here, Sizaal?" Mezzy asked.

Sizaal looked around. There were barely two dozen humans in this group. *We are to defeat the yurdrakon* and *Pra'tear? I fear for our chances.*

"I require your assistance," Sizaal said. He opened the earth below them and let what he brought with him rise to the surface. Everyone jumped back in alarm, and some reached for weapons as Tem's unconscious body rolled to face the night sky.

"What is… *that thing* doing here?" the man named Evan asked.

"I wish to cure him," Sizaal replied.

"You should destroy him!" Evan said, but Mezzy raised her arm in deference.

Milo turned somber at the sight of Tem. "You did something to him," Sizaal said, as he turned his focus on Milo.

Milo stood and nodded. "I did."

"You accept your mistake. Good. Now you will help me cure him. Your technology is preposterous and beyond my understanding."

Milo took a step forward, then looked to Mezzy.

"Apologies, leader Mezzy. It is of the utmost importance I cure this one," Sizaal pointed at Tem. "It is a condition Neema required of me before she would see the guardstone."

"It's not Neema's decision to make."

"It was not this boy's decision to be made into this abomination."

Mezzy looked away. Sizaal felt the tension in the camp like the ground beneath his feet.

"He was cured once before," Evan said.

"He was *not* cured. What was done to him released the pressure in his mind, but it gave him more power than he could handle. I will relieve him of that pressure once young Milo removes the device that hinders him."

Mezzy thought for a moment. "I will oversee it. If he makes a move toward any of us at any moment, I'll kill him myself. Don't think I won't."

"Agreed. I've already prepared a chamber. Follow me." Sizaal led them to a rock formation just outside of their camp.

"I want guards at this exit," Mezzy said. "If he comes out before the rest of us, kill him."

"It will not come to that." Sizaal clapped his hand on Milo's shoulder. "Little man, are your nerves calm?"

"Yeah, sure," Milo replied. "I'm going to operate on this kid with a talking tree. That definitely isn't affecting my nerves."

"The tree is merely a part of me. I am many things."

It had been a generation since Sizaal reported on the effects of elemental manipulation on humans. *Everything I ever tried proved inconclusive. What did Pra'tear do to these people?*

Sizaal set Tem down on a flattened slab of rock. "We'll begin immediately. Remove the collar."

"Yeah, you got it," Milo said, and he started dismantling the device.

"Wait!" Sizaal said, noticing something. "Are those wind shards?"

"Mhmm. It was the only way to secure the water stone. See?" Milo pointed inside.

"Interesting." Sizaal grew tiny pincers on the ends of his fingers and secured the wind shards in place. "Now remove the collar."

Milo did so, letting it fall to the rock while Sizaal felt around the elements at work within Tem's body. "There's something else here."

"Is anyone else cold?" Evan asked. Sizaal hadn't noticed, but the temperature had dropped significantly.

Mezzy shifted on her heels. "What's going on, Sizaal?"

"Patience, young woman!"

Sizaal felt the elements igniting with energy inside Tem. *I must hurry!*

There, attached to the water stone within Tem's neck, Sizaal felt a mind stone. *Why would you force control over the humans in this way, Pra'tear?* Sizaal dismissed ever using mind stones during his research, because the Essence cost was too high. *Unless one has an endless source of Essence. Then an entire race could be enslaved if enough mind stones were obtained.*

Tem stirred, and Mezzy gripped her knife tighter. He would wake at any moment. As soon as-

Snap!

The air in the cave below freezing in an instant. Tem's eyelids opened to reveal glowing white eyes, and he arched his back, screaming.

I've got it! Sizaal grasped the mind stone, pulling it from the back of Tem's neck.

Energy burst from the boy's body, pushing Milo, Mezzy, and Evan away. Mezzy got to her feet and tried crawling toward Tem, her knife still in hand.

With a burst of Essence, Sizaal mended the remaining elements inside Tem by, using tiny vines and repairing any damage the mind stone caused.

"Wake up, boy!" Sizaal yelled.

A moment later, Tem fell back to the rock slab, quiet and unmoving. Mezzy's knife was at the boy's throat.

"No!" Sizaal cried.

She held the blade there, waiting for any sign of danger. Tem winced once, then opened his eyes again. This time they were a calm blue, like the ocean on a clear day.

"Who are you?" Tem asked. "Where am I?"

"My name is Mezzy, and you're not going anywhere until I say so."

"What have I done? The last thing I remember is being with Neema."

Tem's eyes went wide. "Neema! Where is she!?"

"Your lover friend is okay, small Tem," Sizaal said. A blush crept up on the boy's face. "She is attaining a weapon to defeat Pra'tear, false king of the humans, your former master." *She should have joined us by now. What happened to her?*

Tem shook his head. "You can't beat him. I don't care what powers you or anyone else has. This world *bends* to him. The only thing we can do is run."

"Hiding is not living," Mezzy said. "If what you both say is true. The king will not stop until all of humanity is enslaved, or worse. You can hide in the rocks, the jungle, the Deadlands, wherever, but as powerful as he is, he *will* find you. The only thing we can do is fight. *Together*."

Sizaal nodded. *She has confidence. That is good.*

"We leave for Essence City," Mezzy ordered. "I have some arrangements to make when we arrive."

*****

Neema fought, but no matter what she did the barrier remained.

I have enough Essence to blast to the center of the world, but I'm stuck here!

All that would get through the barrier were useless shifts in the elements. *Whatever good that does me.*

She could feel the presence of the yurdrakon, and what it carried. *A life stone. The power to change.* She knew what it was by sifting through the knowledge Arlac bestowed upon her. With that, Pra'tear would end humanity for good.

He doesn't care about breaking the rules of the world. This power is too much for anyone or anything to control. Even now, Neema sensed the

Essence trying to escape her body.

In the darkness, Neema tried to think about the choice Arlac said was coming. She feared that no matter what choice she made she would still lose.

*****

For the first time in years, Tem's mind was clear, free of the menacing presence that infected him since he was young. Even when he was awake for that short period with Neema he could feel it in the back of his mind, pulling at his sanity. Now it was gone.

I feel... normal!

The world was brighter. Even in the dreary outskirts of Essence City there was a beauty that was absent for too long. The air was warm and refreshing. Tem breathed in deep, looking up at the sky.

The rebels he travelled with kept their distance. Tem couldn't blame them. He remembered hurting their friends, people they loved and cared for. It was like waking up from a terrible nightmare.

Essence City peaked over the next rise, its buildings stretching toward the sky. At the foot of the hill, crops stretched for miles until they hit the city walls. Tem had returned to Essence City multiple times since he was reborn as a mindless. He watched his body walk the streets from the back of his mind, recalling all the places he'd been, but not able to take himself to the places he really wanted to go.

"Everyone stay tight," Mezzy called back. "Don't wanna run into any mindless patrols."

"I don't know how you're feeling," Milo said, clapping Tem on the shoulder, "but I trust Neema, and she trusted you, so now I trust you." The man's grip tightened. "I *trust* you won't let me down."

"I hope so," Tem replied.

"That right there is enough for me, son."

"Let's go, you two!" Evan said. He led them through the corn fields toward the city. "Hurry up!" They rushed, ducking as they ran.

How are we supposed to get inside? Tem thought.

Mezzy turned into a low grown corn row.

I sure hope a patrol doesn't come by, he thought, feeling exposed out in the open so close to the city.

"It's right up here," Mezzy whispered.

That's when Tem saw them. A firemind and a stormmind, heading straight for the rebels.

Tem ignited the two elements inside of him, noticing how weak they felt compared to before. "Go!" he yelled. "I'll take care of them."

Mezzy turned and nodded, waving everyone on.

He felt the heat before it hit him, so he instinctively surrounded himself in a ball of water. Through the waves, Tem saw the stormmind grin.

I'm at a disadvantage!

Lightning flashed, and Tem was just able to use his wind power and fly out of the way.

"Now it's my turn!" he yelled, raining down on them with a barrage of water blasts.

They countered and began a back and forth exchange of water, wind, fire, and lightning. A searing heat hit his side, sizzling and charring his skin. Then electricity zapped his arm.

I need more power!

He dug deep, using everything he had to conjure wind and water together. Ice built up on his arms, chest, and legs, and Tem's breath was visible as it left his lips. Neither mindless soldier reacted to his abilities.

Of course they wouldn't, he thought. *They aren't* allowed *to fear.*

With a fistful of ice, Tem pounded the firemind into the dirt, leaving the young man unconscious. The stormmind let loose, bombarding Tem with multiple lightning strikes. Before Tem was able to fight back, a resounding *crack* filled the open field. The stormmind dropped to the ground, motionless.

Tem landed next to the young man and looked up to see Mezzy holding a pistol.

"Why would you do that!?" he cried.

Before she could answer, a blistering heat surrounded them. Tem didn't have to turn to know the yurdrakon was descending upon the city.

"We gotta go," Mezzy said, looking high in the sky. "Come on! Come on!" She pointed to a slit in the ground, barely large enough for him to slide through. "In here."

He regarded her with a gaze as cold as the ice falling from his hands, but he ducked inside the passage.

"Straight ahead," Mezzy said.

Tem had to feel his way along the dirt walls, stumbling over crude, wooden beams that kept the place from caving in. They walked at least a hundred meters in silence until they met a small ladder at the end of the tunnel. Light poured from above.

"Nowhere to go but up."

Above, Tem squeezed in with everyone else while Mezzy worked her way to the front of the room.

"Is this someone's basement?" Tem asked. Above the crowd, he noticed a tall, portly man at the foot of a set of stairs.

I know that face, he told himself. It was the power stone merchant from the market Tem and Neema stole from all those years ago. *This day gets better and better. I wake up from one nightmare and enter another. Hope he doesn't recognize me.*

"You know I support the rebellion, Mez," the merchant said, "but I think we should all get out of here while we can. If that thing destroys the city, I'll have nothing left to support you with."

"There's nowhere to go, Abraham. The king or the monster, whoever wins will raze this city and its people to the ground. We have to stop them both."

Abraham's face was filled with sorrow, but he replaced it a moment later with determination. "However I can help then. I have these you can use." He handed off a few weapons.

Mezzy nodded, then led the party upstairs. As Tem walked by Abraham, the man looked at him with curiosity. He looked as if he wanted to say something, but merely furrowed his eyebrows.

The ground shook, and the walls buckled. Dust rained from the boards in the ceiling.

There's no more time. He pushed ahead to the front of the group and got Mezzy's attention.

"Whatever you have planned, I'm sure it doesn't involve me," Tem said. "Find Neema and the talking tree. I'll be fighting that monster."

Tem took to the winds before Mezzy could respond.

Chapter Fourteen

Neema waited in the cavern, surrounded by gloom. The yurdrakon was upon Essence City. It would terrorize it in its battle against Pra'tear and the mindless army. There was nothing she could do, even though she understood so much more about her powers.

If only I could access them outside this damn barrier! she thought. *Pra'tear has been waiting for this day for a century! I just got thrown in yesterday.*

A noise echoed in the chamber, interrupting Neema's thoughts. In the darkness, she couldn't see the source of the noise or feel anyone's presence. *Pra'tear?*

Neema braced herself. If he was here to finish her off, she would fight with everything she had! She writhed and wriggled, trying to free herself in a last ditch effort to take a stand.

But it doesn't make any sense! she thought. *The yurdrakon is still alive. I can* feel *it! Why would he come back now?*

Footsteps drew closer, pounding, pounding. Neema inhaled, breathing in the damp cavern air.

"Jessii?" she called.

Jessii's silhouette appeared in front of Neema. How could Jessii have found her? Jessii rushed closer, studying the barrier.

Wait, Neema thought, watching Jessii's facial expressions. "You understand. Don't you?"

Neema altered wind, earth, and water, just enough to form a sentence in the library of elements at Neema's disposal.

Jessii nodded, urging her to do more.

"I've tried! It doesn't do anything."

Jessii crinkled her nose, as if telling Neema she better do what Jessii insisted.

"You're a lot more talkative than I remember, girl."

Jessii rolled her eyes, then moved in a way that raised Neema's eyebrow.

"How did you…" Jessii was reaching *inside* the barrier! "Okay, yeah! Yeah!" Neema continued shifting the elements, and Jessii responded by inching further and further inside, peeling away each layer.

Pra'tear created it without thinking those tiny shifts in the elements would find their way through. He had big thoughts, focusing on the big picture, but Neema was different. She was always the little one. She came from stealing chips in the market to fighting in the rebellion. *This* was what she knew.

Jessii seized Neema's wrist. It was warm and sweaty, but filled with life. Life that Neema had been disconnected from, but it flourished over her all at once. The barrier would not restrict her anymore, nor would it dissipate. It would remain in the cavern.

Have fun with your empty prison, asshole.

*****

Sizaal had never been inside the city before. It reeked of garbage and human waste.

"What happened to the elements here?" he asked. "It is as if they weep continuously." Was this Pra'tear's doing? Or the humans?

Any plants nearby were withered and dying, the air was polluted, and the rain, once so fresh and new, was contaminated before it reached the ground.

Sizaal silenced the cries along the way, releasing little bits of Essence where he could on his way to the palace.

Pra'tear will be there. Sizaal hoped to convince him one last time to end the torturous game he played.

The streets were empty in this part of the city. Of course, Pra'tear wouldn't let the humans live so close to him. Some mindless abominations flew by on their way to fight the yurdrakon, but Sizaal steered far from them. Sizaal looked up and saw the buildings billowing smoke into the air, corrupting it with toxins.

"This must end. It all must end. The world weeps, yet no one listens."

The palace was grand, as Sizaal expected it to be. A pristine white wall surrounded it, but Sizaal cleared it in a single jump. Inside the outer wall there were dozens of temples dedicated to Pra'tear. Each temple told a story.

Lies! Pra'tear filled the humans' minds with fables of his conquests to power. He claimed he freed them from the clutches of tyrannical gods.

That freedom came with a cost. The mindless army. Pra'tear forced the humans to fight against the yurdraks. A false price paid for slavery.

I will show them true freedom.

The silver, gold, and gemstones that lined the temple walls glimmered in the rain. Royal guards patrolled the premises, but Sizaal clung to the shadows. The palace itself rested upon a hill within the walls, overlooking all of Essence City. From there, Pra'tear would watch in amusement as the yurdrakon decimated the city.

Only one entrance inside the palace. I will have to fight my way in! A pair of royal guards stood at the end of the bridge leading to the massive palace doors.

Using his wind heart, Sizaal burst forward. The two guards reacted quickly. *They're infected!* Sizaal realized, sensing the presence of power stones inside the men. The power stones made them much stronger and faster than a normal human.

"I will free you!" Sizaal said, extending his arm into a spear and striking the first guard through his heavily armored chest. Blood seeped from the wound, splattering both Sizaal and the remaining guard.

That guard didn't bat an eye for his fallen comrade, attacking Sizaal with a frenzy he hadn't seen from a human before, mindless or not.

What have you done to these men, Pra'tear!?

Before the guard could land a blow on Sizaal, the sanctor engaged his earth heart. He manipulated his body and limbs to wrap around the human, slowly crushing him like a snake constricting around its prey.

"Now you are free."

Two more guards must have heard the scuffle, because they emerged from the palace with halberds at the ready. Sizaal retracted his arm back into a fist and ran at them. The guards separated, trying to flank Sizaal.

"That won't work against me." As Sizaal ran, he reformed his body, growing a pair of arms from his backside.

An even fight!

He spun at them in a flurry of wood and rock, dancing between, around, above, and below them as more blood gushed, painting the bridge in dark red.

Sizaal braced himself for what lay beyond the door. He retracted his two new arms and tightened his body, threading wood and rock together until Sizaal was half his normal size.

"I need to be stronger and faster if I am to fight more of these atrocities," Sizaal told himself.

The doors boomed open to reveal a large entry chamber. Lanterns were lit inside, bathing the stones walls in orange. At the far end, a grand staircase twisted either way to the great hall above. On the staircase was a platoon of royal guards and mindless soldiers.

He ran toward them and jumped high, nearing the chamber's high ceiling. In an explosion of Essence, Sizaal ignited every element within him. He slammed back to the ground like a meteor, killing the royal guards and mindless soldiers in one incredible shot. When he stood, the chamber floors were smoldering and dark. The palace was silent.

Before he took a step, the palace walls broke inward. Then they collapsed again in a dizzying and mind-bending experience. Again and again they collapsed upon themselves. Suddenly, the movements stopped, and Sizaal was on his knees.

"So, you've come," the voice above him said.

Sizaal couldn't return to his feet, no matter what he tried to do. Nor could he raise his head or alter his body to see where he was.

I am in Pra'tear's presence.

"I've waited a long time to see you again, brother," Pra'tear growled. "It's a shame it had to come to this."

"Don't let it!" Sizaal said. His words were strained and muffled. Pra'tear's grip on Sizaal was breaking his body.

"Are you trying to play the positive role for these infectious humans?

Make them believe you can free them from the bonds that I hold? It is useless." Pra'tear let go of the elements surrounding Sizaal. Sizaal stood on a red carpet lined with silks and linens. Pra'tear sat upon a gold throne that overlooked the city.

"Look, old friend." Pra'tear pointed toward the open wall that led out to the city. Beyond the skyline, Sizaal saw the yurdrakon in battle with the mindless army. Lava spewed from the beast and rained down to the streets. "It's beautiful isn't it? It's taken generations for me to understand that an evolved yurdrak can generate enough Essence to form a life stone. I will kill it and become whole."

"You cannot do this!" Sizaal cried. "You must listen to me!"

"No, I mustn't. You don't know what I do, Sizaal. You don't know what I've done to save everyone! You've allied yourself with these humans, but they don't even know what you are. What you've done. What you *wish* to do."

"No-"

"SILENCE! The time has come. I will do what I must to regain my true form, even if it means I must destroy you."

Pra'tear rose from the throne and walked toward Sizaal. He raised a hand, and Sizaal felt his chest rip apart. Wood chips and rocks fell to the floor as Pra'tear exposed Sizaal's hearts. Sizaal knew pain, but what he felt now was unbearable. Pra'tear was ripping him apart piece by piece.

"You can watch while I slay that creature. Then I'll bring that pathetic girl back here and kill her too. Be thankful, Sizaal. You will be the last being to witness this age, before I build the world anew… in my image."

Pra'tear yanked away Sizaal's remaining Essence, cutting him off from the world.

*****

Tem rose above the city. Below, the yurdrakon attacked the mindless army.

I need to go higher!

He flew even with the clouds and away from the heat. Only then could he gather enough strength to take it out. Tem concentrated his energy, closed his eyes, and blanketed himself in the wind.

I've felt this before, he thought. *It happened while I was under the king's control.*

"Come on, Tem," he told himself. He still feared the depths of his power, but he needed to control it long enough to unleash one devastating attack and kill the yurdrakon. "I don't know what the king wants with it, and I don't care, I'm gonna beat him to the punch!"

The air around Tem crawled, and the clouds turned to ice. Shards of ice orbited him as he looked down at the monster. The very air and clouds around him filled his elemental stones with Essence. Then he fell.

The wind whipped at his face. Tem focused on the shards of ice, they drew more water from the clouds and grew. Tem reached further inside of him, tapping whatever power remained. He yelled, but the noise was lost in the descent. It took all his concentration to keep control of himself and the weapons he commanded. The shards were larger than him, but in the eyes of the yurdrakon they were merely daggers.

Tem let out one last cry and launched the shards towards the beast. It was unaware of the icy death that rained from above. Right when the first ice blade pierced the beast's back it cried out and toppled a nearby building.

The other shards followed, though the heat from the yurdrakon's lava weakened them.

"Now the big finale!" Tem reached out next to him, grabbing the last ice shard. He fashioned it into a sword longer than him, hoping it was strong enough to penetrate the yurdrakon's thick, rocky shell.

He looked down, meeting the monster's gaze. Its eyes were ablaze and centered on Tem's own. A heat blast shot upward, making Tem sweat, but he poured his energy to maintain the strength of the sword. He raised it above his head, and with the force of the winds he swung down.

The blade punctured the beast's snout, pouring lava across the ground. Tem had to keep the winds beneath him to stay clear of it. He let go of the blade, and it slowly melted away, but the damage it caused was done. The yurdrakon did not move.

"I did it!" he said. "I won!"

A dozen mindless looked on, and Tem tensed. He'd almost forgot.

The king… he'll be coming. Tem looked around. "Love to stay and chat with ya, fellas. But uh, I gotta grab somethin from this thing here, then I'll jet! Yall don't mind, right?"

If he struck fast and hard, he could take out half of them, then work on the rest before the king arrived. He formed ice daggers in each hand, the power in his elemental stones nearing depletion, and planned out his next ten moves. Before he could implement anything, smoke poured around him. He turned around, and through the haze two searing, demon eyes stared back at him. The yurdrakon was still alive.

"Impossible," Tem muttered. The word escaped his mouth as a blast of lava shot forward, sending him down the block. Tem tried to cover himself with ice, but the attack was too strong. Lava burned through his armor, scalding his skin.

The yurdrakon stood, and Tem watched the hole in its snout reform with new molten rock.

"What's it gonna take to beat this thing?" To stand was more effort than he could generate, and he didn't have enough energy to form ice.

Winds rippled above him, taking the yurdrakon's attention away from Tem. An airship swooped in and blasted the yurdrakon with a continuous stream of cannon fire.

It hovered low, blocking Tem's view of the yurdrakon.

"Is that... Mezzy?" The young woman was at the airship's helm, and Milo and the others were with her. The constant barrage kept the yurdrakon busy while the rebels debarked and joined the fight.

Rebels and mindless alike fought the creature like drops of water against raging flames.

"You good, son?" Milo appeared at Tem's side, helping him to his feet.

Tem nodded. "Never thought I'd see this. Rebels and mindless fighting together."

"You'd be surprised what can happen when faced with a common enemy."

"What happens when that enemy is defeated?" Tem asked.

Milo smacked Tem's butt. "We'll figure that out after we beat it."

By Antonio Baldari

*****

The airship was harder to steer than Mezzy anticipated. It had been built by the rebellion as a last minute evacuation plan. Mezzy repurposed it with an automatic turret. She strafed back and forth, firing on the yurdrakon.

"I feel like all I'm doing is pissing it off!"

It launched fireballs, boulders, and splashes of lava at Mezzy, but she hadn't been hit yet. The few soldiers that manned the turret rocked and swayed, but they held on and kept firing.

"You boys good back there!?" she called.

The only response was a steady stream of cannon fire.

"I'll take that as a yes."

The earth beneath the yurdrakon shifted, and rock slabs emerged from within, shielding the monster from Mezzy's aerial assault.

"Shit!" she cursed. If they lowered within sight of the yurdrakon, it would have dead aim at destroying the ship. "Can't risk it."

Where was Neema? Sizaal said she should have met up with them hours ago, and she was the only one with the power to defeat it.

I'm worried about Jessii, too. After Sizaal arrived, Jessii disappeared without a trace. "Can't worry about her yet."

"Ma'am!" one of the soldiers called. "There's an opening toward its hind leg! If we swing around we could hit it there!"

Mezzy nodded and turned the airship around. The pounding cannon continued its onslaught, but Mezzy had a feeling deep in the pit of her stomach that it made no difference.

*****

The heat from the yurdrakon made Milo's breath weak and his face drip with sweat. There was nothing he could do to attack it, so he stayed back and helped the wounded. Right now, the most important wounded was Tem. The boy's body was burned, bruised, and battered. Even his eyes looked tired and faithless. He was also their only hope.

"Tem," Milo said, "you are the difference."

Tem shook his head. "I hit that thing hard, and it's still up and fighting. Even harder than before. That was everything I had!"

Milo spat. "Boy, I saw you turn an entire camp to ice with the snap of your fingers. I'd never been so cold my whole life!"

"That wasn't me."

"But that power was!"

Tem looked away. "Not since I've woken up. It's not as strong, and I've used everything I had."

Milo grabbed the boy's shoulders. "Nothing has changed. You still have the same elements within you, the same power! The only thing is now they are *yours*, not his. Feel those elements around you, boy. The wind. The water. They're yours!"

Tem looked past Milo to the beast behind them. It wouldn't be long before the annoyances of the other rebels and the mindless were silenced. Tem was their only hope.

"Dig deep, the power is there, don't be afraid of it. Control it!"

Milo grabbed Tem's face and looked him in the eyes. After a few moments, Tem nodded.

"Go get it, kid."

Tem stepped away from Milo as wind and water funneled around him. Ice encircled Tem until he was covered in a set of shining armor. Without turning, Tem said, "You should get somewhere safe."

Milo raised his arm, shielding himself from the strengthening winds.

A sword formed in the mist around Tem, along with a shield, great helm, and wings of crystalline ice.

"Control it!" Milo yelled as Tem flew away.

This fight was no longer one that could be fought with rifles or gauntlets or airships. Milo took on a new mission.

"I will make sure no one else gets hurt." There were plenty of rebels, mindless, and innocents that could get caught up in this battle of man versus beast. While Tem was at odds with the yurdrakon, Milo sprinted across the battlefield toward where Evan was lining his sights from a rooftop.

"Evan!" Milo yelled. "We need to get everyone out of here!"

Evan didn't respond. He was too busy firing at the yurdrakon.

How does he not see how useless it is? Even with his water infused bullets, they would have no effect on the yurdrakon.

"Damnit, boy!" Milo cursed. "Just don't die."

The constantly changing temperature had Milo sweating one second and shivering the next. Up ahead, a small group of mindless soldiers huddled next to a building, mending their wounds before rejoining the fight.

They wouldn't listen even if I tried, Milo thought. The best he would get from a mindless soldier is an elemental blast to the face. Young men were so quick to lose their lives, whether their minds were controlled or not.

"What am I going to do," he muttered, looking up at Tem fighting the yurdrakon. It was a terrible and beautiful thing to watch. The boy landed a blow with his sword against the monster's cheek, but the cut merely spilled lava and reformed. The yurdrakon retaliated, but Tem blocked the flaming boulder with his ice shield, sending it into the side of a building.

There, Milo noticed a man huddling with his family under the crumbling building.

"I can make it!" Milo started to run. *Maybe Mezzy can come by and pick them up; take them to safety.* Evan was making his choice. The mindless followed their orders. Milo would save this family.

Ice rained from the sky, stabbing the ground ahead. Milo jumped and slammed his gauntlets together, creating a shockwave that cleared his path to the family.

"Come with me!" he called. "I can get you out of here!"

The man looked at his wife and child, then turned to Milo and nodded. He was an older man, his wife much younger than him, and his daughter not even a dozen years old and shaking in her mother's arms.

Milo checked his radio to get in contact with Mezzy. It clicked but couldn't transmit. The only way to contact her would be with a flare.

Can't risk that, Milo thought, knowing it would only draw unwanted attention.

Milo could still hear the airship's cannon pounding, echoing down every street. Mezzy wouldn't stop the barrage for a flare.

"I know a way! Come!" *I will save them.*

*****

Tem didn't know what he was doing. It was like his body moved on its own. Years of training bound his muscles to fight. He froze a flaming boulder solid and shot it back to the yurdrakon. It hit the beast's shoulder and bounced off.

It was dizzying. It was intense. It was terrible.

I'm alive! he thought.

Power surged through him, and it was like he was a kid running through the market again. He laughed as he sliced through a stream of lava with his ice sword and batted away the remaining splashes with his shield. He pressed on, slashing at the monster. Everyone around him disappeared.

It's just me and you!

It lifted a paw to swipe at him, so Tem put everything he had into a concentrated ice beam. The ice froze the lava and crawled up the yurdrakon's front leg. Tem clenched his jaw and dug deeper. The monstrosity's foot halted midair. Without even thinking about what he was doing, Tem churned wind around his hand in the form of a spinning disc. There were windminds that could carve rock and even metal with their powers. Tem threw the wind disk, and it sliced through the leg, sending it crashing to the ground where it shattered into tiny pieces.

Tem didn't stop, reaching further into the emptying abyss of his powers.

It's now or never!

The very air around him thickened and fogged. The yurdrakon's fire dimmed. It tried to attack, but Tem deflected everything thrown his way. He flew closer and closer, then raised his arm and yelled. The power within him swelled, nearing its breaking point.

"STOP!"

Tem barely heard the cry, but a second later his powers were gone.

"What?" he mumbled. Then he looked to the sky. He had to shield his eyes, because he saw something that he never thought he'd see in Essence City. It was the sun.

Clouds parted to reveal a blue sky, and a figure descended. "Neema!?"

She was accompanied by someone, Tem wasn't sure who, but he didn't care.

Behind him, the yurdrakon emitted a quaking growl.

Oh shit, Tem thought, forgetting about the yurdrakon. "Neema, NO!" Tem hadn't paid attention!

Neema walked right up to the yurdrakon with her hand raised like she was going to pet it. Strange enough, the beast didn't attack. It shook its head, but Neema shifted her arms slightly and the beast bowed to her.

"You won't hurt anyone anymore, will you?" Neema said, her voice was as sweet as jelly. She patted it on the snout and turned to Tem.

She looks… different. Her eyes were brighter, hair smoother, and cheeks full of life. He looked down at himself and blushed. His armor was gone, and all he was left with was torn rags for clothes.

"What did you do?" he asked, surprised that he was able to form words.

"I healed her."

"*Her?*" Tem did not understand anything that was going on.

"I've awoken, Tem. There is much more healing that needs to be done, and we don't have a lot of time."

Chapter Fifteen

Neema looked out over the decimated remains of the upper city. Craters of ice and molten rock dotted the once magnificent upscale skyscrapers where the city's wealthiest lived.

I need to know my friends are okay, she thought. Everyone's presence was close by, but she couldn't pinpoint them.

"There's Evan," she said to herself, spotting him on the roof of a nearby building. He hopped down and headed toward her. Mezzy was flying around in the airship, hovering cautiously around the yurdrakon. Neema communicated that update to Jessii, whose face flushed at the news.

"Where's Milo?" she asked, not finding him anywhere.

"He was with me before I started fighting the yurdrakon," Tem said. "It's all kind of a blur after that."

Evan shook his head. "I haven't seen him lately."

Neema cursed. Milo's help would be useful right about now. *Pra'tear wants the life stone. I have to get it first!* She would have to try to extract the life stone from the yurdrakon on her own. There was no more time to waste.

"Find Milo!"

Before she turned away, a blinding flash followed by an earth shaking roar stopped Neema cold.

Oh no... She knew what happened before her eyes could confirm it. *I'm too late!* A hole where the blast hit gaped open at the top of the yurdrakon's head, then a giant rock blade split its skull open.

King Pra'tear descended, followed by a stream of dark clouds. Neema dispelled his curse from the city earlier, but wherever he was it followed.

"Monster!" Neema cried.

The king merely laughed.

I could have saved it! I could have cured it and released it back to its base form. The elements twisted the draks into devastating creatures of immense power. Pra'tear's reign is what corrupted those elements to turn so chaotic.

She understood him now. Everything he did was to torment humans. *Why does he hate us so much?*

"Thank you, little girl. You made it so easy for me to take this life stone." Pra'tear's grin was menacing. "I don't know how you escaped my prison, but now I won't have to travel back so far to kill you."

"You can't kill me!" Neema grinned. She had a few tricks up her sleeve too. While he was talking, she communicated with Jessii to retrieve the life stone. *Just gotta give her a distraction.* Fortunately, with all of her new powers at her disposal, that was the easy part.

Neema flew toward him, filling her fist with a multitude of elements. She struck him square in the jaw, but it did little more than knock him back a few inches. It was like he wore an armor of wind to keep her from hitting him.

Two can play that game! Electricity sparked and crackled around her, zapping anything nearby.

The two combatants settled on the ground, staring at each other for the briefest of moments. She got his attention, now she needed to keep it while Jessii inched her way to the yurdrakon.

"This is pointless, human," Pra'tear murmured. "Even with Arlac's Essence, you don't possess the knowledge or experience I do."

A burning sensation throbbed inside her pants pocket, the feeling making her aware of something. The darkness surrounding them wasn't just because Pra'tear made the clouds return.

We're in the middle of an eclipse. The sun and the moon!

She pulled the eclipse stone out of her pocket, and a striking light flashed across the city. The Essence within the stone forged it into a sword. Its hilt as dark as a shadow; its blade as radiant as the sun.

For a mere moment, Pra'tear's eyes widened.

"Are you afraid of a little girl, Pra'tear?" Neema gave him a devilish smile. "A mere *human*?"

Pra'tear growled, but Neema didn't give him a chance to answer. She screamed and swung the sword of absolute Essence at the former sanctor. The power she wielded scared him.

"Where did you obtain that weapon!?" he questioned, barely dodging her strike.

Neema continued attacking. "A little gift from Arlac!"

"Rahhhhh!" he screamed, trying to blast her with attacks from a host of different elements. She parried them all away with the sword and advanced on him again. "That cursed rock continues to be a thorn in my side!"

"Take this!" He attempted to shield himself, but she sliced his forearm, leaving a gash from his wrist to his elbow. When Pra'tear lowered his freshly scarred arms, Neema witnessed a menace she had never seen before.

"I'm done playing with you, *insect*." His voice was low and sinister. "Kill them all," he ordered. The several mindless soldiers engaged the remaining rebels and the hovering airship.

"No!" Neema yelled. He still had the number advantage! In a flash, he appeared in front of Neema and smacked her with the back of his hand, rocketing her across the street into a building wall.

Their fight had only begun.

*****

"Neema!" Tem watched her skid across the ground and crash into the side of a building. As he tried to help, a contingent of mindless soldiers blocked his path and surrounded him.

"You wanna fight!?" Tem yelled. Neema's grip on his elemental powers was gone, so he summoned an ice sword and dashed forward, slashing at his enemies.

It was strange. He recognized some of these men. Some of them went through training with him, went on missions together, fought and bled together.

Can't think of that right now! He stole a glance in Neema's direction to make sure she was okay, then continued fighting. *I won't let you die, Neema. I won't let anyone die!*

*****

Neema and Pra'tear exchanged blows. She was beginning to understand the depths of her power, and with every second that passed she gained the upper hand.

The fear she thought she saw earlier was apparent in his eyes, only making him more dangerous. His attacks were frenzied, chaotic, and *powerful.* She'd held this power for a day. He'd held it for a generation. He knew how to form and release Essence in so many ways.

Come at me, Pra'tear! I'll make you pay! She used sheer force combined with the eclipse sword to block and counter his attacks. And it was working.

He tried confusing her senses by altering the space around them, but she retaliated by altering it back and to the opposite. They fought in night, day, rain, heat, upside down, and inverted. It was like they were in a world of their own making.

"It's over, asshole!" Victory was within her grasp. In seconds, she'd have his head.

Pra'tear's face curdled from fear and anger to smug arrogance. The world around them returned to normal, and Neema had to stop herself from tearing out Pra'tear's throat.

Something's wrong... There was a presence that was different from before. She looked down and saw why.

Braden stood on the ground, looking up at her with a knife to Milo's throat. A small family stood nearby, surrounded by mindless. All around the city block, the rebels were defeated and held captive by the mindless soldiers. Their battle was lost.

Pra'tear smiled, filling Neema's chest with rage and heartache.

"Give me the life stone, child, and I'll let them live," he demanded. "Consider it a token for a well fought battle." Pra'tear raised his voice for everyone to hear. "I am your god! And I will show mercy on these traitors at the *sacrifice* of their leader."

"Liar," Neema muttered.

Pra'tear inched his face closer to hers. Close enough that she could smell his putrid breath, making her stomach turn. "I don't need your approval. I already have everything!"

She noticed too late. Mezzy's airship swarmed with mindless, distracting Jessii. Her diverted gaze gave Pra'tear the moment he needed to seize control of the life stone. Neema didn't have time to alter its path, the wind carried it straight to Pra'tear's outstretched hand.

"Finally!" Pra'tear yelled. His hand was no longer flesh, blood, and bone, but rock, wood, and metal. He was returning to his sanctor form. "My curse has been lifted! And now you all shall *suffer*!"

What do I do? she asked herself. Even with her Essence and the eclipse sword she wouldn't be able to stop him. With the life stone he could do unimaginable things. Horrible things.

"Is this the choice I have to make, Arlac?" She looked down at Tem. He stood with a handful of mindless soldiers at his feet, looking up at her with those big, blue eyes.

Even though he couldn't hear her, she still said to him, "I love you." Tears welled as she then turned to the king. "Pra'tear! I told you I'd make you pay!"

His transformation was complete. It was time.

"Neema, no!" Tem cried from below.

Neema let the power within her swell. It boiled, slowly ripping her body apart. In moments, it would ignite, releasing enough Essence to lay waste to the sanctor. And herself.

*****

Light flickered around Neema. Somehow, Tem knew that whatever she was doing would be the end.

I won't let you do this! Not after everything he'd been through. Not for him. Not for anyone. If anyone deserved to live, it was her. *I have to do something!*

"Everyone! On me!" he yelled, then flew straight toward the king.

*****

Evan didn't care that it didn't make a difference. A small gnat buzzing in front of a giant still distracted the giant.

I have to help somehow, he told himself. *This is what heroes do!*

He would not roll over and go quietly into servitude.

Evan lifted his rifle, aimed, and fired.

Braden fell to the ground. Milo jumped into action, knocking out two of the mindless soldiers holding the captive family, while Evan dropped the others. Milo nodded in his direction, then they both turned their sights on Pra'tear.

*****

"You think you can kill me?" Pra'tear asked. With a motion of his hand, everything stopped. Bullets, spears, and rocks hung in the air, Neema tried to move closer to him, but she was trapped in a similar barrier to the one in the cave.

She screamed as the little strands of Essence worked their way to the surface like they were clawing their way out of her body.

I can't stop it, she thought, knowing her attempt to kill him was in vain, *and now I'm going to die.*

*****

"Pra'tear!" Tem called, using all of his power to inch closer and closer to the king. "I won't let you hurt her!"

The king smiled. "But who's going to stop me from hurting *you*?" He raised an arm and Tem felt his insides twist. An excruciating pain erupted in his skull.

Bad idea!

"Fight me!" Tem cried. "Fight me like a man!"

The king's smile turned to a frown filled with disgust. "I am no man, *boy*. I am a *god!* And you will bow before me!" Tem felt his knees buckle, and he was forced to drop. The king floated forward and looked down at Tem. "You love her, don't you?"

Tem clenched his jaw.

Pra'tear looked at Neema, his smile returning. "You'll watch as I kill him. You pitiful humans…"

Tem noticed something just then; slight shifts in the air, leading straight to Pra'tear like a tunnel.

Tem grinned his old mischievous smile. When Pra'tear turned his features twisted into disgust.

"What are you-"

Tem blew a stream of wind through the makeshift tunnel, knocking the life stone from Pra'tear's grasp and sending it straight to Neema.

"NO!" the king cried.

Neema plucked it from the air and rolled it through her fingers, batting her eyelashes at the king. "I'd ask you how it feels," she said, "but I really don't give a shit."

In the next instant, a blinding light flared from Neema's hands. Tem thought he heard her scream, or was that him? Or Pra'tear?

When Tem's vision returned, he was lying on the ground in a crater the size of his old apartment building. Neema stood above him. At first, he thought it was the sun, but it was behind him so it couldn't have been.

"Are you... glowing?" he asked Neema. "Wait, where's-"

The king was gone.

"Did we win?" Tem asked, rushing to his feet. "We did, we won! We won!" He cheered, calling for the other rebels to join in. "The king is dead!"

The remaining mindless soldiers had fallen to the ground, unconscious.

"They'll be fine," Neema said, as if she knew what Tem was going to ask. "I've cured them."

Tem hugged her, and as their skin touched, he felt the immense power she held. "Are you okay, Neema?"

"It's not over, Tem," she said, her eyes looking into his, but it was like she was somewhere else entirely.

"What's going on?" Milo asked as the others surrounded them.

"This is... too much! I can't hold it! This power is too great for anyone to hold. It must be kept safe."

"Where's that?" Evan asked.

Neema shook her head. "I don't know, but I know someone who does."

She took off, blasting away faster than Tem could register. He followed the airstream, leading straight to the palace. His muscles ached from pushing his body and powers past their limits. Flying was so taxing that he almost passed out on the way.

Neema! He caught a glimpse of her crashing through the massive front windows and pushed on, forcing himself to stay conscious.

He landed in a pile of broken glass. *Is this the throne room?* His question was answered when he turned and found Sizaal leaning against the immense, gilded throne.

"Pra'tear is dead?" Sizaal asked.

Neema nodded.

"You hold the Essence now."

"Yes," Neema said.

"And you know what you must do."

"But I don't know how. This power is too great and too dangerous for a human to have."

Sizaal nodded. "It's good you came to me. I don't have much time."

"I can heal you," Neema cried.

Sizaal shook his head and dried leaves crumbled to the floor. "I am beyond healing, even with your power. I was created by the elements, serve the elements, and die by their command. A new age is dawning, I'm afraid."

Neema nodded, somehow understanding Sizaal's words.

"Here," she said, holding out her hand and revealing a sparkling bead. It was relaxing to watch, and Tem had a hard time peeling his eyes away. Sizaal took the bead and placed it inside his open chest cavity. Neema exhaled, relaxing as if a heavy burden had passed from her, and Sizaal's eyes brightened like stoked flames.

"I will reshape this world," Sizaal said, his voice hoarse.

"How?" Neema asked.

Goosebumps trickled up Tem's spine as Sizaal continued. "Pra'tear was wrong to enslave humans. I see now! The balance must be restored. The balance, Neema!

"What are you talking about, Sizaal?" she asked.

The sanctor swayed his head back and forth, staring into some far off place.

"The elements weep for what has been wrought," Sizaal said. "I will free you to restore the balance. Yes, I see."

"Who?" Tem asked. "Who needs to be freed?"

Sizaal turned to Tem and Neema then, one at a time. When he spoke, he wasn't in the distant place he seemed to be before.

"*Humanity*," Sizaal said.

Tem's eyes went wide, and Neema gasped.

"The burden you place on the elements is too much. The world weeps for the damage that has been done. I must correct it now."

Immediately, Tem's insides burned with a fire hotter than the yurdrakon's breath. Neema screamed and curled over in pain.

She can't fight it!

Tem tapped what water and wind power remained, encasing himself in ice. He dropped to one knee, hoping to last long enough to do something, anything, against Sizaal.

"Can't you see?" Sizaal said. "You are ruining this planet! To save it, you all must die!"

Tem fell toward Neema. He ran his hand through her hair. She was burning up. "There must be a way to stop this!"

Neema could barely raise her eyes to meet his. She motioned to Sizaal and the open void in his chest.

Tem nodded, understanding. The Essence needed to be destroyed.

I can do this, Tem thought, trying to block out the extreme pain coursing through his body. *I don't know what I'm doing, but I know Neema believes in me. That means I can do it!*

Tem's ice began to melt, and his vision hazed. It was now or the end. He lunged forward, his muscles and skin feeling like they were peeling away, and then grabbed the energy.

Someone screamed. This time he knew it was him.

Everything around Tem stopped. He entered a space beyond the world and away from the palace. Tem floated in the never-ending black, feeling the power of the world all around him. It was intense. Overwhelming. Strengthening. This was what being *alive* felt like! The power was all he needed, and with it he would control everything.

A thought in the depths of his mind bubbled to the surface.

I was supposed to do something.

Tem couldn't remember what it was, but he knew that it was good and beautiful and loving. The image of a familiar woman arrived in his mind. Who was she?

She's the reason I'm here.

She needed him to do something. Something unthinkable.

I can't give away this power! Why would I ever do such a thing!? He had tried to obtain a power like this his entire life. Now that he had it there was no reason to give it all away. Everything he ever wanted was within his grasp!

"Tem, please…"

The voice was barely a whisper. Tem. That was his name. For those few moments he was beyond names. He just was.

Neema? I must do this for her. For everyone!

That's when he heard the elements. They were strained to the point of breaking. Sizaal was right. The constant abuse over the centuries pushed them to the very limits, and if they continued down this path, the world would soon see its demise.

But there's another answer, Tem realized. It was so obvious it was a wonder he didn't realize it before. *This power… it's stolen!* Tem searched the Essence's memories, confirming his suspicions. *This is what Pra'tear found. The guardstones stole the Essence from the elements.* It needed to be returned!

Tem flexed the power, pushing, bending, cracking. The Essence was distributed all over the world as elemental stones, forcing the elements into a chaotic form of slavery. Tem tightened his grip.

This is too great for humans, sanctors, or guardstones. Nature knows how to keep balance on its own!

The Essence snapped, and it was like a floodgate had been opened. It left him like the breath from his lungs after a sucker punch to the gut. Then the power and space around him shattered, leaving him in nothing.

His time in this place was nearing an end, so he felt for the elements. Nothing responded, even the stones embedded in his body. Nothing. The elements were finally free.

When Tem opened his eyes, he was lying on the throne room floor. The ceiling above him was adorned with the same gems and precious metals as the rest of the building. Neema was to his left, but Tem couldn't see her eyes through the hair that had fallen in front of her face. The quiet whisper of her breath and her chest rising and falling gave him comfort that she was alive.

"Unhh," Tem groaned. Sizaal sat still against the throne, and Tem knew he was dead.

In a way, Tem understood what the sanctor tried to do. When Tem held that power, it overwhelmed him enough that he wanted the same and more. The power, and any control over the elements, was something far too great for anyone or anything to possess. Tem felt again for water and wind. Nothing.

I could get used to that, he thought.

A nearby rustle caught his attention. Neema brushed her hair back and watched him. She smiled, filling him with a better feeling than control of any element could have given him.

"Did we win?" she asked.

Tem scooted closer, wrapping an arm around her and pulling her close. "Yeah, we won."

Epilogue

Neema sat on the edge of the docks, swinging her legs above the water. The sun shone overhead, and a salty breeze kissed her face.

"You look happy again, Neema," Milo said. He placed his hands on his hips and took a deep breath.

"I'd like to think we all do," Neema said, standing and nodding to where the others waited for frozen suisu treats. "So what's next for you? Botany?" Neema smiled.

Milo chuckled. "Something like that. I think I'm going to help out here in the city first. Lots of people gonna need it. Ya know?"

Neema nodded. "Hey, Mezzy!" Neema expected her former superior to scowl and try to turn away at the sound of her call, but instead she grinned. "You get one for me?"

Mezzy stuck the suisu treat in her mouth, then plucked it out and held it toward Neema.

"Never mind."

Jessii snuck by, stealing the snack and winking at Neema. Then she grabbed Mezzy's hand and pulled her to the dock.

"What about you?" Neema asked Evan.

He slugged her in the shoulder as he passed by and turned out his pockets. "Sorry, Neema. I'm broke!"

Neema sighed and walked backwards, bumping into Tem. "Oh! Hey, you."

He held up an extra suisu. "I remember owing ya one."

She took it and licked a little piece dripping down the side, savoring the sweet flavor. "I'm pretty sure I still owe you, but I can forgive you. Everything still normal?"

"If by 'normal,' you mean powerless but completely happy? Then yeah, all good over here." Tem bit a large chunk of his fruit, chomping it down. "I went and saw my pa today."

"How was that?" Neema asked.

Tem looked out toward the water, his eyes still the prettiest blue Neema'd seen. "He spit out his drink when he saw me, then it took an hour convincing him I wasn't some drunken illusion. Your folks?"

"I saw them too. They're good." Neema led him along with the others at the dock.

"Hey, Temmy!" Mezzy called. "My friend, Abraham, has agreed to help out a bunch of your mindless pals. Givin em jobs at the market, that sorta thing. He asked about you, but I told him you'd probably be busy with other things."

Tem looked at Neema and smirked. "You'd probably be right, but thanks. Knowing that means a lot."

The group stood in silence aside from the slurping and splashing waves for a few more minutes. Neema finished her suisu and tossed it in the garbage. "I think that's it for me. Gonna head to the palace. I hear there's some big meeting going on. Figure I can go keep everyone in line and make sure whoever's put in charge isn't some genocidal tyrant." She winked and walked off, but before she made it very far Evan called out to her.

"Neema, wait! You should see this."

She turned, expecting a prank or joke, but everyone was facing the water and peering over the dock's edge.

"What is it?" she asked.

"Look!"

Out on the horizon, a ship cruised toward Essence City. Even from that distance, Neema could make out the massive, black sails.

"Essence City doesn't have ships that big," Tem said, his grip tightening on the dock rails.

"So who are they?"

Absolute Essence | Christopher Guhl

Christopher Guhl is a science fiction and fantasy author raised in Des Moines, Iowa. He graduated from the University of Iowa with a bachelor of applied studies and an emphasis track in creative writing. His first novel, *Naevia-18*, released in 2018 (Autumn Arch Publishing). When not writing, he enjoys cosplay, breakdancing, and spending time with loved ones. Christopher lives in Iowa with his wife, Candy, and their little dog, Charlee.

ACKNOWLEDGMENTS

This was such a fun book to write! It stemmed from my love of fantasy role playing video games, popular anime and manga titles, and embarking on crazy adventures with crazier people.

First off, I'd like to thank my wife, Candy, for believing in me, pushing me, and keeping it real. Without you, I wouldn't have the courage to produce stories like this.

I'd also like to thank my family and wonderful friends. It's because of you amazing people that I enjoy stuff like this, and hence want to write my own stories!

I need to give a special shout out to Mr. Aaron Bunce. You've pushed me to be a better writer at every step of my writing career. I look forward to our growing friendship and your continued mentoring. Thank you, sir!

My advanced reader squad! You all are the real MVPs. You keep me from making a total fool of myself! Thank you, Autumn Nelson, Camille Valley, Chakong Vue, Jarod Meyer, Sara O Delp, Somchit Mongtin, Tayla Fazio, and William Rock.

I'd also like to thank the amazing artists I've worked with on this novel. Thank you, Artauxeo (cover artist), Covers by Christian (cover letterer), Antonio Baldari (interior illustrator), and my fan artists, Patrick Yin and Dean Hoang Van.

And thanks to you, lovely reader! I hope you've enjoyed my story. Keep turning these pages to see some super cool fan art and a sneak peek at my next novella, *Descent (Karxen Chronicles Book 1.5)*!!!

Absolute Essence | Christopher Guhl

Neema by Patrick Yin

Absolute Essence | Christopher Guhl

Jessii by Christopher Guhl

Absolute Essence | Christopher Guhl

Yurdrak by Dean Hoang Van

DESCENT

Chapter 1: Fire

"Naev!" Zoë cried, trying to pull her pants over the cast on her leg. Naevia was already out the door and out of sight. Zoë limped to the doorway and watched her disappear into the distance, a cloud of dust trailing her. *It wasn't what it looked like, Naev.* Zoë thought to herself.

"Way to go," the voice said from behind her. Raina.

Ugh, Zoë thought. *Of course she's here to make me feel worse.*

Zoë looked at her, then returned to her bunk. "Whatever," she muttered.

Kyler emerged from the back room, his bodysuit partially zipped up on the sides. Naevia couldn't blame Zoë that she was curious, could she? It's not like her and Kyler were *doing* anything.

Zoë wasn't looking, but could feel Raina standing in the doorway, staring at her.

"You just gonna stand there or what?" Zoë asked.

"I'll do whatever I please, which appears to be exactly what you do." Raina responded.

What is that supposed to mean? Zoë asked herself. "Oh please, don't worry about her. She'll blow off her steam and come back later. You can oogle all over her then, so don't get your panties twisted."

"Umm," Kyler said, "if I can interject?"

"No!" Zoë and Raina both yelled. Zoë leaned back in her bunk and rolled over, hiking up her pants in the process. *Stupid pants, stupid men, stupid women. Ugh. What has my world come to? This was supposed to be easy. Walk around, kick some rocks, the Outside was supposed to be our answer to a boring city.*

"Guess I got my wish," she muttered to herself. "Nothing boring has happened since we left Karxen."

Stupid me, she thought, *for not knowing the training exercise Stephanie brought us out on was really the beginning of a coup.* She snuggled into the warmth of her blanket, but it snagged on her cast.

"Rrrr!" she growled. "Stupid leg!" She tossed the blanket up and shook it out, freeing her leg. The Outside sun was coming in right through the barracks window, so Zoë rolled back over and hid beneath her blanket.

If Naevia wants to run off and pout that's fine. I'll get some shut eye and forget it all. Zoë started dozing off, trying to put the remaining ache in her belly out of her mind. She was just about to fall asleep when the sunlight twinkled against her eyelids.

"Hm?" she startled herself awake. The barracks were empty, but she could've swore there was movement from outside. "Naevia? Is that you?" Zoë stood and shuffled her way to the door.

"Go! Now!" Raina yelled from across the courtyard. Kyler was running toward the tower.

What's going on? Zoë thought.

"They're coming!" Raina shouted. "Get back inside, Zoë!"

Bette emerged from the building, and darted her head back and forth at Raina and Zoë. Her eyes settled on something in the distance, past the tree-line. Zoë squinted and tried to follow. There were shapes within the forest, moving quickly.

"What is th-?" Before Zoë could finish a group of soldiers erupted out of the forest. Zoë gasped and slammed the door shut, retreating back to her bunk.

"What do I do? What do I do?" With her leg broken she was useless in a fight. The commotion outside built with intensity. In a moment, Raina and Bette both barreled through the door to the barracks.

"It's no use, Raina," Bette said. "We're outnumbered."

"Not if I can help it!" Raina shoved an empty bunk against the door, then pulled a rod free from another bunk, tossed it to Zoë, and grabbed another for herself. "Let's do this! Numbers won't matter in here!"

Zoë nodded, unsure that she'd be able to do much with her broken leg, but she stabilized herself near the wall. *I won't go down without a fight,* she told herself. *Not this time!*

The window behind her crashed open, shards pouring to the

floor like rain. Zoë yelped and ducked her head down, but no one was there. A ball the size of her fists bounced across the floor, spewing dark smoke that began masking the surroundings within the barracks. The door to the barracks pounded.

"Get that smoke outta here, Zoë!" Raina yelled, trying to keep her weight against the bunked jammed into the door.

"Hm!" Zoë limped her way to the smoke bomb, just as another crashed through the other window. "Ah!" she yelled. She tried grabbing them both to throw them out, but they burned to the touch. Zoë grabbed a nearby sheet and wrapped them together. "Yes! I got it!" Zoë lifted the bulging sheet up victoriously.

Just then the sheet ignited into flames, and Zoë screamed, tossing the sheet towards the window. It hit the windowsill with a crunch, and the flames trickled from the window to the walls and nearby bunks.

"What happened!?" Raina yelled, and just then she was thrown off balance as the door to the barracks splintered open. Women in all black bodysuits poured into the barracks, and Raina sprang from the floor to the nearest one.

Zoë reached back and grabbed the metal rod, then jumped off of her good leg to the nearest soldier. She swung the metal rod and landed a hit on her shoulder, shoving her to the side to swing for the next one. Just as she reached back to strike again one of the women shot at her, two darts plunging into Zoë's abdomen. In an instant, Zoë's muscles tensed and burned like fire, and she dropped to the floor. She was sure that the drop would hurt, but she couldn't feel anything through the raging energy that pulsed through every muscle in her body. She strained to look up from the floor. Raina was on top of a soldier, but she got struck with the same weapon and her limbs straightened as she dropped to the floor. Bette was already restrained and on her knees.

What happens now? Zoë asked herself. *What have we gotten ourselves into?* Then she remembered, *Naevia! Naevia can fix this. She can fix anything.* As Zoë fought against losing consciousness she could feel herself being drug on the ground as multiple hands grasped her. The red sun from the Outside beamed down on her and everything faded from red to black.

Chapter 2: Confinement

Zoë stormed back and forth in her cell. There were a multitude of healing wraps on her leg, but it still hurt to walk. She didn't care. *Who does Admin think they are?* She thought. *Why should they be able to control us?*

"You can't control me!" she shouted at the wall. "If I want to take a stroll in the Outside, I'm gonna do it! And if I want to co-host the nightly news with Emilia I'm gonna do that too!" Zoë slapped the wall with her open palm, and pain shot through her hand, tingling every nerve and tainting her hand red.

She slumped to the floor and blew whatever hair she could out of her eyes. Things stayed like that for awhile. In a few hours, a tray of food slid through an opening in the door.

"Hey!" she yelled. "Get back here and fight me like a woman!" She looked down at the tray of food and cringed. "Really? Brussells sprouts? Yuck." She kicked the tray away with her good foot and leaned back again.

Hours passed until Zoë heard the door sliding open again. "Is it time for dessert?" she asked.

"No," a voice answered.

I know that voice, Zoë thought. A chill went down her spine as she sat up and stared at Naevia's mother, Dericka, the second most intimidating woman in Karxen. *Oh, shit.*

Her hair draped over her shoulders in black curls, and her bodysuit was spotless. Zoë looked up at her like she were a small child that had just been punished for eating too much dessert. She'd been in this situation before, numerous times, but now it was like Naevia's mother was an entirely different person. Her chin was held higher, hands balled into fists, and dark lines were etched beneath her eyes.

"Where is my daughter?" Dericka asked.

Zoë clenched her jaw like that would help keep her from speaking.

"Where is she!?" Dericka asked again, louder this time.

Zoë turned away this time, her eyes navigating to the corner of the room furthest from where Dericka stood. Dericka walked over, her steps clicking along the tile floor. She knelt down and grabbed Zoë by her chin, forcing her to look into Dericka's dark, bottomless eyes.

Dericka didn't need to say anything. Zoë wasn't going to let her bully her. No, not her. All Naevia's life, her mother bullied her into doing whatever she wanted. If Naevia wasn't going to stick up for herself, Zoë was going to do it for the both of them.

"She went to the Outside," Zoë said, staring into those deep, brown eyes, "and she *loves* it! There's nothing you can do to stop her from telling everyone in Karxen your dirty little secret."

Dericka's lips pursed, and she said matter of factly, "I could kill her."

Zoë's eyes widened, but she kept herself from drawing in a deep breath. *She's just trying to scare you, Zo. That's all.*

Dericka ran her hand along Zoë's cheek, the tips of her nails grating against Zoë's skin. Dericka grabbed one of Zoë's pigtails and ran her thumb through the bright green hair. "Or I could kill *you*. How much does she *really* love you, Zoë?"

Oh you wanna dance, huh? How about this? "More than a mother that never approved of her," Zoë spat. "Not all of us were fortunate enough to be assigned to a single mother like Naevia was, but I'm glad I was with my group. They pushed me to pursue what I wanted! And in doing that it pushed Naevia too, because we're sisters."

"Hmph," Dericka snorted. "You know nothing, little Zoë. You are the way you are because of me, as is Naevia. I could kill you and replace you without a second thought, and Naevia wouldn't even know the difference."

"That doesn't even make any sense!" Zoë yelled. "What are you-"

Dericka held up a finger to Zoë's lips, silencing her. "You're dedicated to her. I get that. Now let me think. I'm certain we've caught most of your rebel group. Naevia is probably out there, leading a meager squad to our gates in attempt to free you and the others. She'll have friends in Karxen that might help her, and she might cause a slight uproar. She won't succeed though, no. This entire city can change overnight. That's something none of you realize. Everyone could wake up tomorrow leading entirely different lives." Dericka stroked Zoë's chin and cheeks, her eyes darting to different spots in the room like she were thinking things over in her mind. She seethed, then nodded. "Yes. This should work, but she'll need help."

"Are you crazy?" Zoë asked.

"Something like that, but I've made up my mind. I'm certain things will work this time. If not, all of Karxen is doomed. Come, Zoë. I need to show you something."

DESCENT (Karxen Chronicles Book 1.5) will be available soon from Paper Star Publishing! Check **ChristopherGuhl.com** for the latest updates!